BEACHFRONT SECRETS

SOLOMONS ISLAND BOOK 6

⚜

MICHELE GILCREST

Copyright © 2022 by Michele Gilcrest

All rights reserved.

No part of this book may be reproduced in any form or by any electronic or mechanical means, including information storage and retrieval systems, without written permission from the author, except for the use of brief quotations in a book review.

GET A FREE BOOK!

Would you like a FREE book? JOIN Michele's newsletter to receive information about new releases, giveaways, and special promotions! To say thank you, I'll send you a FREE copy of The Inn at Pelican Beach. Sign up today!

https://dl.bookfunnel.com/wr9wvokoin

CHAPTER 1

Mackenzie Rowland perused the aisles of the grocery store with her dear friend, Clara, filling her buggy with essentials to last her another week. Unfortunately, their summer schedules were growing increasingly demanding now that tourist season was upon them. But this Sunday, that didn't stop them from making time for each other, even if it meant catching up over a thirty-minute run to the store.

"Should I try the grape jelly or strawberry preserves?" Mackenzie asked, holding up the store's featured items of the week.

"Go with the preserves. Whenever they feature one of our local's homemade products, it's always a hit in my opinion. The grape jelly will always be there if you don't like it."

"Good point, my dear. Good point. So — tell me. How are things going with you these days? You know it's rather pathetic when you have to schedule a date at the grocery store to play catch up with your girlfriend. One who works right across the street might I add." Mack teased.

"Tell me about it. I can't remember the last time I came over to the café to have lunch. It truly has to stop. I miss your company and I miss catching up with the regulars."

"We miss you too, love. How's married life treating you? Are you and Mike ready to start having a boatload of babies?"

Clara's eyes bulged. "At forty-nine? By the time I reach seventy, my kid would be almost twenty. Not impossible, but not exactly what I had in mind. The thought of adopting an older kid that needs a home has crossed my mind a time or two, but I don't know, Mack. It may not be in the cards for us at all."

"And that's fine," she said, reaching for a box of cereal. "You'll know if it's meant to be."

Clara cleared her throat. "What about you and Brody? Is everything okay with you two?"

"As far as I know. I mean, things have been a little tricky ever since Stephanie's father reemerged into our lives. But, for the most part, I think we're fine. Why? Do you know something I don't?" Mackenzie asked.

Brody and Mackenzie had been together for a couple of years, with growing intentions of getting married someday. He jelled well with her daughter, Stephanie, who'd just turned seven, and would give Mack the world if she asked him to.

Clara shook her head. "No, I was just wondering. It just seems like he's awfully quiet lately. I used to catch him rattling off to Mike all the time about his plans with you. Now, I hardly can get a peep out of the guy. Men are weird. Who knows? It's probably nothing."

"Hmm. You're right, I'm sure it's nothing," Mack said, brushing it off. Although, internally, she had an inkling of what it was. Ever since Stephanie's father reemerged into their lives, things were shifting between her and Brody in a strange kind of way. Since she didn't know how to balance her and Stephanie's renewed relationship with her father, and Brody's connection with her, she sort of didn't address it at all. Probably not the wisest way to go about it, but she was doing the best she could given the circumstances.

"How's everything going with Stephanie and her father? Have they been spending time together since his initial call back in April?"

Mack skimmed over the meat section, carefully considering the selections and her words.

"Yes. One would've thought with him being a part of a band that he wouldn't have a lot of time to spare. But he's proven just the opposite. In between his shows at the Harbor, he's made plenty of time for her, driving down and meeting us at various locations. It's been kind of shocking, actually."

Mackenzie could feel Clara staring, waiting for more of a reaction, but she wasn't quite sure what to say. She was still trying to figure it out herself. She never understood how a man could allow his passion for music to override his responsibilities and cause him to walk out and leave. But, according to him, that was years ago, when he was young, naïve, and irresponsible. Now he's back, supposedly seeing the error of his ways, fulfilling his commitment to at least visit with Stephanie, and standing by his word. She didn't know what to make of it.

"Earth to Mack. Are you there?"

"What did you say?" Mack asked.

"I didn't say anything. I was waiting to hear more from you. You hadn't mentioned anything about their visits, which is not like you. How is everything going between them? And how does Brody fit into the puzzle? I'm sure this has to be a bit awkward for him."

"Do you think?" Mack asked. "Ben is Stephanie's father. While I'm still struggling with the idea that he just woke up one morning and decided he wanted to be in her life again... he's still... her dad. What was I to do? Tell him sorry, you lost your opportunity at being a father a long time ago when you left? Or, better yet, tell Stephanie someday when she's older? Oh yeah, by the way, your dad did make several attempts to be a part of your life, but I told him to go fly a kite." She chuckled defensively.

"No, of course, you wouldn't do that, Mack. I totally think you're doing the right thing, no matter how hard it might be. I was just wondering where Brody fits in, that's all. He's very attached to Steph, and cares about her as if she was his very own. Maybe that's why he's been so quiet lately. Perhaps the guy just needs some reassurance in his role in all of this."

"Maybe. If that's the case, then we'll have to talk about it. But, for now, the only thing on my mind is enjoying a relaxing afternoon with him while we wait for Stephanie to return from her camping trip," Mack replied, feeling a little tension in her neck.

"I'm jealous. I have yard work to do this afternoon. Your plans sound way more fun." Clara chuckled.

Mackenzie's cell phone rang with an unknown number flashing across the screen. While thoroughly engaged in picking out the perfect sauce for her pasta meal, she mashed the green button, in case the call had something to do with Stephanie.

"I should take this. Excuse me for a minute." She explained. "Hello?"

A deep voice replied on the other end of the line. "Mackenzie."

"Ben?" she said, instantly regretting that she said his name out loud.

"Yeah, it's me. Do you have a minute?"

"I'm in the middle of grocery shopping if you're looking to speak with Steph. She's on her way back from the camping trip I told you about. She won't be back until at least three-thirty."

"I can't wait to hear about it. But I actually called because I wanted to speak with you."

Her eyes peered over at Clara standing a few feet away with a box of rigatoni in hand.

"I'm listening," she said.

"I'm considering making a decision soon that will impact all of us. Unfortunately, I'm having to operate under time restraints with an impending trip to Boston for a concert. I have to act fast on this decision before I hit the road, and if there's any chance you could pull yourself away for a few hours... and maybe meet up with me this afternoon... it would mean the world to me. I think it's something we should discuss in person and not over the phone."

Again, Mack checked for Clara, then pushed her cart further away. Under her breath she mumbled, "Ben, I'm not sure what you're referring to, but surely you can make your decision without involving the rest of us."

"Mackenzie, I promise it's positive, and it's coming from a good place in my heart. I owe it to you and Steph to continuously prove that I'm not going anywhere. To show you that you can trust me again. Please, just meet with me. I have a meeting this morning and then the afternoon is wide open. What do you say?"

A quiet moment passed as she watched Clara approaching with her cart.

"Please?" he begged.

"Okay. Text me the location and time. I gotta go."

She then mashed the red button, ending the call, not wanting to look suspicious to Clara.

CHAPTER 2

Brody knocked on Mackenzie's apartment door while hiding a bouquet of roses behind his back. He figured maybe he could surprise her and squeeze in some alone time before her daughter returned from her camping trip. It would be the perfect end to the weekend. And a wonderful way to spend quality time with his lady. It seemed kind of childish to him, but when they weren't together, he longed for Mackenzie, daydreaming about their next kiss. For him, it was one of the telltale signs he was falling deeper in love.

"Brody?" she said.

"Mack." He jumped, startled at her approach. "I thought you were inside. I came over a little early to surprise you," he said, allowing the flowers to rest at his side. As he looked down, he noticed she was tugging several bags filled with groceries, so he grabbed as many as he could.

Mackenzie stepped forward. "I guess I got carried away talking to Clara. There's no such thing as a thirty-minute shopping trip when you're with your girlfriend. It's darn near impossible."

She unlocked the door, and he followed her in, placing all the bags on the counter.

"I'm glad you had a chance to see Clara. These are for you, by the way," he said, handing her the bouquet.

"Thank you, Brody. You didn't have to spend your money on flowers," she said.

"I know, but I wanted to. To say that I've missed you over these last couple of days would be an understatement. With you working shifts at the café, and me putting in extra hours, I feel like our time together has been limited. I've missed you," Brody replied, then leaned in to taste the sweetness of her lower lip, then gently retreated.

He smiled at the sight of her standing still, puckering up her lips. "I take it you don't want me to stop?"

"No, and that's the problem. Whenever we're around each other, it's hard to peel away," she said.

Again, he dove in, this time for a full mouth-to-mouth session, leaving his pulse racing and heat rising from within.

After a moment, Mackenzie took a turn, gently pulling away, leaving him wanting more. "If we keep this up, my frozen goods are going to melt. Stephanie will never let me hear the end of it if she doesn't have ice cream tonight for dessert. I'll have to make sure I tell her it was your fault." She teased.

"Well, in that case, let's unpack the groceries. Speaking of dessert, I was thinking we could spend the afternoon together, then pick up Steph, and maybe grab some dinner together. How does that sound?"

"Well."

He noticed Mackenzie's hesitation. "I don't want to be presumptuous. If you already have plans just let me know."

"It's not that. I'm still scheduled to meet her at three-thirty, but prior to you surprising me, I was actually going to call to ask for a rain check for this afternoon. Something important came up that I probably should handle," she said.

"Oh. Is everything okay?"

"Yes, everything is fine. It's just... well, you know how it is. As you said, it's been so busy lately. Trying to take care of things during the week is almost impossible, so I figured I'd squeeze in an important errand. We could all grab dinner after if you'd like."

Brody balled up the remaining plastic bags, tossing them in the trash. "Sure. No problem. It was probably foolish of me to come over early without calling first. Sometimes I get these bright ideas and just run with it, not really thinking it through."

"Brodyyy. Come on, don't say that. Bringing the flowers over was very sweet."

Something felt off to Brody, but he couldn't put his finger on what it was. It wasn't like Mackenzie to refuse a spontaneous, romantic afternoon. She usually craved their alone time just as much as he did.

"So, this errand of yours. Is this a solo thing or do you think there's room for a tag-along?" He chuckled.

"I highly doubt you'd want to tag along for this. It's rather boring, actually." She slipped her arms around his waist. "What do you think about Steph and I meeting you later on? Let's say around four at the new Italian place off of Main Street? I can even call and make reservations."

"Uh, sure. Four o'clock it is." He gave her a peck on the forehead, quietly hoping he had done nothing to warrant the sudden shift.

"I was kind of hoping at dinner we could have a talk, collectively as a team, if you will," he said.

"About what?"

"I've been thinking, if you agree, maybe it's time for us to talk with Stephanie about us becoming a family in the near future. You and I have been on the same page about this for a while, and we're pretty clear about the direction we're heading in. But, it might be nice to give Steph an opportunity to express her feelings about the matter. I don't think we've ever created an opportunity for all of us to sit down and talk about it together."

He could feel Mack's hands subtly slip away, and a serious expression washed over her face.

"Brody," she said, holding her head down. "I think timing is everything. While I agree with you it's an important discussion that we all need to have, I don't know that now is the right time. I mean, how much can a young girl handle at once? She's just getting used to the idea that her dad is back in her life, and all she can seem to talk about is when she will get to see him again and how cool it is that he sings in a band. Somehow, I think if we spring too much on her at once, it may not go over so well."

"Okay. I guess I hadn't considered that aspect of it. All I see is a happy-go-lucky little girl who appears to be thrilled when we're all together. It never crossed my mind that the conversation would be too much for her," he replied.

"Well, it might be."

"I'm not trying to overstep my boundaries, but have you considered that it might not be? I'm not suggesting that we spring a proposal on her. But, I would like to plan for one at some point. The more we talk about sharing our lives together, don't you think she should be a part of that conversation?" he asked.

"Yes, I do. But, again, it has to be at the right time. On her terms. If you think about it, we were living our everyday lives, clueless that Ben would just resurface, turning our world upside down. All of this is going to take some getting used to, babe."

Brody walked over to her window, glancing at a pedestrian

crossing the street. "I'll support your decision and won't say anything until you are ready. After all, you're her mother and you know what's best for Stephanie."

Outwardly he said all the right things, but internally he hoped the goals they had for their lives together weren't changing. And, if they were, he hoped she would tell him.

∼

Around midday Brody returned to Lighthouse Tours to make himself useful. With a heavier load of tourists coming through, he figured he'd get a head start on the mechanical checklist for the week, keeping himself occupied until four o'clock.

He pulled his set of wrenches off the shelf when the owner and his best friend, Mike, entered the room.

"Brody, what are you doing here on a Sunday afternoon?" he asked.

"Hey, Mike. Figured I'd get a head start on a few chores for the upcoming week. The earlier I can complete my to-do list, the earlier I can head to the North Beach office this week."

"Ah, yes, North Beach. I talked with our secretary, Jan, earlier. Don't be surprised if she doesn't have a list of her own waiting for when you return." He chuckled.

"I'm sure she will. I'll check in with her first thing on Monday morning."

The room fell silent as Brody continued to fidget with his tools. He could sense Mike watching him. He was probably wondering why he wasn't being his usual talkative and bubbly self, which was so out of character. But, since Brody couldn't even explain it, he hoped Mike wouldn't ask.

"The tours have been picking up like crazy. Tommy and I had two earlier this morning, with at least one more scheduled for this afternoon," Mike said, attempting to break the silence.

"That's good."

"Yep. Tis the season." Brody shifted around, looking for another tool set.

"You alright, man? You don't seem like yourself today," Mike asked.

"Yeah, I'm fine. Just focused, I guess."

"Mmm. Not sure I believe you, buddy. We've been hanging tough for years now. I'd like to think I can recognize when something is wrong with one of my closest friends."

Brody offered a lazy smile and switched his baseball cap around on his head, letting it rest backward.

Mike continued. "Come on, man. Let me have it. Are you going through something with Mack? Perhaps a little trouble in paradise?"

"Something like it... I suppose. I don't know, Mike. It's hard for me to read what's going on. All I know is something isn't right," Brody replied.

"Now, we're talking. Opening up and talking about it beats the heck out of keeping things all bottled up inside. Now — not that I proclaim to be an expert by any means, but tell me what's going on. Maybe I can help," he said.

Brody carried a set of keys outside to his favorite boat. It was one of the original boats they acquired when Lighthouse Tours moved to Solomons. Her name was Blue Seal.

"You don't really want to hear about my trivial problems, do you? This is a time of marital bliss for you and Clara. Enjoy it. Don't let the likes of someone like me come along and spoil it with my sad stories."

"Brody, that doesn't even make sense. Talking to me won't impact what I have with Clara. And, just because I'm married now, shouldn't change our dynamic as friends. Now, come out with it. What's bothering you already?" he asked.

Brody shoved the keys in his pocket and turned to face

Mike. "Do you remember the story I told you about my last serious relationship?"

"You mean the one with the woman who —" Mike paused.

"You can say it. The one who I found with another guy. Back then you asked me if I suspected anything or did I have an inkling about it ahead of time. I told you it was a shock to see it for myself, yet on the inside I always felt like something was wrong."

"Yeah. I remember."

Brody continued. "Well, I'm having those same feelings all over again. Except this time, it's with Mack."

"Nooo. Mackenzie? Come on, man. You're joking, right? Mackenzie is an upstanding woman. I don't have to tell you that. She's well-known by everyone as having a stellar reputation, and she's a devoted mother." Mike argued.

"I know, Mike. But hear me out on this. I'm not saying that she's cheating. I don't think she would ever take it that far. But I have noticed that ever since Stephanie's father resurfaced in their lives, there's been a shift or a change in her demeanor. It's almost as if her attention is divided, or maybe even her devotion. Who knows, maybe she's confused. Whatever it is, it's noticeable, and it's giving me an unsettling feeling," he said, resting his foot on the step.

"Hold on a second. You mentioned nothing about Stephanie's father being back in their lives. When did this happen?"

"I thought surely Clara would've shared the news. It's been a few months now. He reached out to her back in the spring, asking if he could talk to Stephanie. Next thing I know, their talks turned into visits, and there you have it. He's back, and although I encouraged her and even supported her through all this, secretly, I'm sorry the guy exists," Brody said.

"Man, you don't mean that. I know you don't. The Brody I

know would want a child to have a relationship with her biological father."

Brody glanced at the subtle wave crashing against the bottom of the boat. Mike was right. He was a good guy, with a good heart, and he wanted what was best for Steph. But he wasn't a fool. This rockstar wanna-be father had resurfaced and was impacting Mack in a way that he didn't care for.

"You're right. It's just my flesh trying to take over, I'm sure. I just don't like the feeling that's been stirring up in the pit of my stomach. Take today for example. We had plans to spend a quiet afternoon with one another. It was supposed to be our alone time before picking up Steph from her weekend camping trip. The Mack I know would jump at the chance of a little one-on-one time. I even went over early to surprise her. But, at the last minute, she changed everything, saying she had to run errands." He explained.

"She doesn't want to spend time with you at all?"

"Well, at least not until this afternoon, after she picks up Steph. Mack would usually give anything for a foot massage, a little wine, and a romantic afternoon for two."

Mike chuckled. "Brody, you two spend too much time slobbering all over each other to be griping about a slight change in plans. One day apart will not kill you. And if I heard you correctly, you're still going to see her later on, which means she still wants you around."

"Laugh if you want, Mike, but I know I'm not way out of bounds on this," Brody responded.

"Okay, let's say you're on to something here. Have you met the guy yet? Maybe that would help put your mind at ease. Better yet, why don't you open up and talk to Mack about how you're feeling? Maybe you need to hear firsthand what she thinks about the whole situation."

"I haven't met him. I figured that's something that

Mackenzie would have to initiate. Right now, everything is rightfully about Stephanie and moving at her pace. The Lord knows I don't want to be selfish. So, I usually just keep my thoughts to myself. I did, however, speak up and say that I thought it was about time we started talking to Steph about taking things to the next level. Getting married had always been the end goal for us. But Mack didn't agree that it was good timing. Again, something that wouldn't be an issue if you know who hadn't shown up."

Mike came over and rested his hand on Brody's shoulder. "Brody, I hate to say something you probably don't want to hear, but it sounds like what Mackenzie really needs right now is your continued support and your patience. She knows how much you love her, and she also knows that you've been loyal. That's way more than the other guy can ever say. Besides, why would she ever want to get back with a man who abandoned her? It wouldn't make any sense."

"Mmm. That's a good point. I guess I sound like a fool for even bringing it up," Brody said.

"No. You just sound like a man who loves her with all his heart and who doesn't want to lose a good thing. But you need to trust her on this one. Don't let something little, like a change in plans, ruin the rest of your afternoon."

Brody revealed a little smile. "As always, you're right."

"I know I am. Now, throw me the keys and let me help you get this bad boy over to the warehouse before it's time for my next tour." Mike chuckled.

◊

After reattaching the hose to the engine, Brody glanced at his watch, deciding it was time to call it quits. He'd much rather go home and shower first than show up wearing oil-stained clothing. He picked up a scrub brush at the sink, applied soap, and scrubbed until his hands were presentable. He then grabbed his keys to head home.

The car ride down Main Street was particularly busy, filled with pedestrians strolling past the shops, taking in the heat of a hot July day.

Brody cranked up the air conditioner while pulling his pickup to a complete stop at the crosswalk. Across the street, he noticed a woman with a familiar frame. From the back, it looked like Mackenzie, talking to a gentleman. But it was probably just someone who looked like her. Intrigued, he continued watching until the cars behind him began honking.

"You're being ridiculous," he said to himself, mashing the accelerator, only to notice as she turned slightly that it really was Mackenzie, and the man she was talking to looked exactly like the guy who showed up at the café one morning. Tall, dark beard, with features like Stephanie, dressed like a rockstar, and who was way out of his league.

Brody pulled over, verifying again that it was her, and contemplating what he should do. Walking up to them like a jealous teenage boyfriend was a surefire way to demonstrate a lack of trust. So, he thought better of it, deciding to wait, figuring Mackenzie would bring it up. Surely there would be an explanation and it would all make sense. At least, he hoped.

CHAPTER 3

Mae Middleton poured a glass of lemonade for her neighbors, Meredith and Edith, before diving into another round of their favorite word game. According to her husband, Jonathan, Mae needed to be more neighborly, more social, inviting the women to come together every once in a while. He said it was what the people of Solomons were supposed to do, and they were no exception.

She wasn't thoroughly convinced this was the only way to be neighborly. Especially since Meredith had a way of always weaving her ideas as HOA president into every conversation. A job Mae thought she took way too seriously. And Edith, who'd only recently learned to call a handyman instead of Jonathan to help with household repairs. Of course, she'd learned to cut her a little slack, given that she was a new homeowner, recently divorced, and still trying to figure out how to make it on her own.

Either way, this particular Sunday afternoon, she extended a warm welcome to both ladies and entertained them on her front porch.

"Would you like a few shortbread cookies to go along with your lemonade, ladies?" she asked.

"I don't mind if I do," Meredith replied.

"Thank you, but I'll pass. I'm trying to watch my girlish figure. I recently started taking walks in the neighborhood. I thought maybe if I wore this silly watch to help with my daily step count, then maybe I can shed a few pounds. I'll never meet a man out here if I start letting myself go." Edith laughed.

"I didn't realize you were in the market, Edith." Mae smiled.

"Ha. Neither did I. And I'm still not certain that's the path that I'm on. One minute I'm fine with being a loner and flying solo. But, night falls and I lie in bed all by myself with all kinds of thoughts running through my mind."

Meredith seemed intrigued. "Are you having trouble adjusting to living in a house by yourself?"

"No, I'm comfortable in the house and I'm very happy with my decision to move here. I just wonder about the future. Sometimes I wonder if I'll spend the rest of my life alone, or since we never had kids, will I grow old with no one to come and check on me every now and then? I know I'm wrong for allowing these kinds of thoughts to creep into my mind, but I do." Edith confessed.

"Edith, I'm sorry you're going through that. When my first husband passed away, I also struggled with similar thoughts. It's human nature. Even though I have my daughter Lily, my son-in-law, and the grandkids, I also feared being alone. But you know what, I forced myself to push past those thoughts at some point. That and anything else that didn't serve any purpose."

Meredith consumed the last bite of her cookie and chimed in. "Easier said than done. Ladies, you don't know lonely until you've walked a mile in my shoes. My son's job keeps him busy traveling here, there, and everywhere. And I've been a widow for over twelve years now. So, the only thing I do to occupy my time is clean the house and —"

"Drive everyone insane with way too many HOA meetings." Mae looked around, immediately realizing she should've used her filter. Thankfully, Meredith and Edith laughed.

"Yes, Mae. I hear you loud and clear. I think it will make you happy to know I plan on scaling back to a quarterly schedule. Who knows, maybe even twice a year, or only as needed. It's time I get out more and start living my life. Just because I'm retired doesn't mean I have to sit at home all day dedicating my whole life to planning for the board." Meredith explained.

Mae's hands flew into the air. "Thank you. It's about time." They all laughed.

Her mind flashed back to this past Thanksgiving when she and Jonathan invited Meredith to dinner. Mae sensed even then that she was lonely. But, she wasn't aware of the depth of it.

"Okay, ladies. The common theme that I keep hearing is that both of you want to get out there and live, without fear, and without regrets, am I right?" Mae asked.

They nodded their heads, collectively agreeing.

"Well, then, let's get you out there. Live a little. Create meaningful experiences to occupy your time. Is there anything that you've really wanted to do, but never got around to it? Now's the time. I'll bet if the two of you sit down at your kitchen tables tonight, you can make a long list of things you've been dying to try. Let's try it now. Close your eyes and see if you can think of at least one thing." Mae waved, encouraging them to go along with her exercise.

Edith raised a finger. "This is easy. I don't have to think long. I've been wanting to take horseback riding lessons since I was in my twenties. But the old bones aren't like they used to be. Another thing I've always wanted to do is go skinny dipping at the beach."

Mae's eyes bulged. "Now hold on a minute. You might want to save the latter idea for a vacation in Rio or somewhere that allows that sort of thing."

Edith and Meredith released a hardy laugh from the belly, allowing them to loosen up even more with each other.

"That's funny. Don't worry. It's just a fantasy. I don't plan on carrying out the second idea. At least not around Solomons Island." Edith chuckled.

"Good," Mae responded.

Meredith cleared her throat, adjusting herself upright in the rocking chair. "I have another confession to make while we're at it. I'd really like to meet a companion. I never thought the day would come where I'd say this, but it might be nice to have someone to enjoy simple things with like sharing a nice meal."

Edith winked. "If I had a man, I'd share more than a nice meal with him."

Mae felt surprised at how comfortable they were airing out everything but appreciated it at the same time. She sensed a common connection between the two. And thought maybe there was something she could do to help.

"You were both married at some point, so I trust that you recall true happiness isn't necessarily achieved just because you have a man in your life. Take me and Jonathan, for example. We bump heads all the time." Mae explained.

"Yes, but at least you have somebody to bump heads with. You two also have a very healthy romantic life — trust me, as your next-door neighbor, I know these things." Meredith teased.

"I have no idea what you're talking about." Mae smiled.

Meredith rolled her eyes, not buying it for one minute. "Mmm hmm."

"Well, I think you and Jonathan make a wonderful couple. You remind me of what I once used to have many, many years ago before the marriage started heading south. Who knows, if it's meant to be, maybe I'll have that kind of love again some day. Except this time, the new and improved version. A version that won't lead to divorce," Edith said.

Mae slapped her leg, darn near knocking over the board to their game.

"I just had a thought. Why don't you guys start going down to the café once a week? Grab something to eat, chat with the locals, and meet some of the people from the bridge club and the bowling league. The only way you can really put yourself in a position to meet someone is to get out there and have fun. You can't do that from the comfort of your own home, you know," Mae said.

Meredith huffed. "Oh, I don't know. I'm not one for playing card games and I stink at bowling."

"Meredith, I didn't say you had to join their clubs. Just go and mingle. Socialize. Expand your horizons a bit, that's all." Mae encouraged.

"I like the idea myself. We should all go one evening for fun," Edith said.

"Well, there you have it. It's a date. I'll even introduce you to the people I know. At least it will be something to get you out of the house," Mae replied.

"To think, maybe my future husband has been dining there all along and I didn't even know it." Meredith laughed.

Mae couldn't imagine who that would be, but if going to the café would give Meredith an outlet, allowing her to let loose for an evening, then she was more than happy to assist.

Mackenzie inhaled the scent of the delicious food, passing along a plate of pasta to Stephanie and Brody. She kept reminding herself to forget about the events of the day and save those thoughts for later when she was alone. Right now, she told herself that she needed to be in the moment, finding out everything about her baby girl's camping trip and spending quality time with Brody.

"Okay, Steph. Brody and I have been waiting all day to hear about your trip. Now that we're all together tell us every detail. Don't leave anything out."

"The trip was so cool. We had a relay race, played duck duck splash, and I had a chance to go in a canoe. We even saw a baby snake, but don't worry, Mom. We yelled for the camp counselors right away." She explained.

Brody smiled. "I'm surprised the boys didn't try to pick the snake up and chase everybody with it."

"Ewe, gross. If someone came near me with a snake, I would scream so loud and run."

Mackenzie laughed. "I'll bet. That makes two of us."

"Do you know what else I really liked?" Stephanie asked.

"What, love?"

"At night all the girls in my cabin got to roast marshmallows while listening to the counselors tell stories. After that, we had free time in our cabin before bed. It was so fun. I really hope I get to do it again," she said.

"We'll have to see. I'm sure if you continue working hard and keep those grades up in school, we can work something out for next summer."

"Yesss!"

Mack glanced over at Brody and his eyes met hers, but they didn't say anything.

"Would anybody like more pasta? The cream sauce is to die for," she said.

"I do," Steph replied.

"Here you go, love. That's enough after you finish what's on your plate. I don't want you to get a tummy ache."

"Okay."

"Tell us more about your trip. So far we've heard about snakes, campfires, and bedtime stories, but you didn't mention anything about meeting new friends." Mack smiled.

"Oh, yeah. I met a new girl named Sarah. She was really nice. I also met another girl named Maeve. We spent the whole time together. Some of the other kids even called us the triplets because we all have the same color hair." She giggled.

Brody chimed in. "Sarah and Maeve. That's wonderful. It sounds like you had a really nice time."

"We did. What did you do this weekend, Brody?"

"Ha. My weekend wasn't nearly as fun as yours, kiddo. But I did get a lot of work done."

"What about you, Mom? Did you have a chance to call dad like you said you would?"

In Mackenzie's mind, everything in the restaurant froze, eliminating everything but the random sound of crickets and katydids, sounding off, waiting for her to respond. Of course, that was only her imagination, but it felt like reality.

"Mommy?"

"Yes, love. What did you say?"

"Did you call dad to ask him if he could come over?" Stephanie repeated.

"I did have a chance to talk to your dad, but he was uncertain of his schedule. He said he'd get back to me," she replied, refusing to look anywhere but at her plate.

"Okay."

In her quiet thoughts Mackenzie was at war over what she

should do. *How did you manage to get yourself in the middle of all this? You might as well say something to Brody. If not, he'll probably figure it out at some point. No. On second thought, take a deep breath and be rational about this. You need to think it through.*

She picked up her fork, clearing the last morsel of pasta off her plate. Internally, Mack was exhausted by her all-consuming thoughts, but figuring everything out on her own was what she did best. She'd always handled everything this way and was used to it after being forced many years ago to make it on her own.

Brody cleared his throat. "You okay? You don't seem like yourself this evening."

She chuckled. "Yes, I'm fine. Perhaps a little tired from running around, but nothing a hot bath can't resolve."

"Yes, that's right. You had errands to take care of earlier. How did everything go?" he asked, laying his hand over hers.

"I was able to get everything done. Thanks again for being so understanding."

She gazed across the table, knowing in her heart Brody was the image of the man she always wanted. Her realistic knight in shining armor. He was loyal, fun-loving, a family man, hardworking. He checked all the boxes and continued checking them as their relationship progressed.

Brody wasn't the issue. The real concern was the re-emergence of Ben, her daughter's father. The man who walked out on them several years ago. He was her former bad boy, turned good. Back then he had straightened up, landing a good day job, promising to be a good husband. That was until an opportunity to be in the limelight came his way.

Ben was her real issue. And, now that he's back, according to her, the rules of engagement should be rather simple. Rebuild a loving relationship with their daughter, keep his promises to her, and not mess up again. Simple, right? No blurry lines to cross or figure out. No memories of the passion they shared when they met and married. No reminders of how deeply in love she was. Right? It sounded easy enough. But, it wasn't. And now he was back with a request. One she didn't know how to handle and certainly wasn't ready to talk about.

"Mom, can I order dessert?" Stephanie asked.

"No, sweetheart. Brody was kind enough to treat us to dinner, but we have ice cream at home."

"It's okay. She can order dessert. You both can," Brody replied, grabbing the dessert menus. "Here, at least take a look and see if there's something you'd like."

She gave the menu the once over, knowing immediately that Steph's eyes would be drawn to the Brownie À La Mode. The kid was a sucker for anything having to do with ice cream and a brownie.

Stephanie's eyes lit up. "Can I —"

"I already know what you're going to say. That's a huge serving for you, young lady. How about we all split it?" she asked.

"Okay."

Mack gently removed a strand of hair out of Stephanie's face, recalling that these were the moments that Ben missed. He had no idea what her favorite dessert was, or her favorite anything, for that matter. Sure, he could learn over time. But, it still gnawed away at her. Hence the back and forth going on in her mind.

Brody placed the order for dessert and then made eye contact with her again, extending his hand across the table. "I'm not quite sure what has you so pre-occupied, but it's something. I just want you to know that I'm here whenever you're ready to talk." Then he addressed Stephanie. "As for you, young lady... I'll have you to know that I absolutely love ice cream. So, you better keep your spoon handy. You never know if a scoop might magically disappear." He teased.

∽

After an evening filled with games with Brody and a little unpacking, Mackenzie found Stephanie hard and fast asleep across the living room couch. The soft music in the background probably could've lulled her to sleep as well. It had been a long day, and she had a lot on her mind. But, those thoughts would have to wait as she prepared to say goodnight to Brody.

"I don't know where you find the energy to play five rounds of checkers, Brody. I swear if I didn't say something, the two of you would still be playing now," she said, shaking her head.

"It worked, didn't it? Look at her. She's completely knocked out on the couch. And, from the looks of things, you should be too."

"I'll get there, eventually. But, first I have to finish unpacking her bags and put her to bed. You know I can't rest well unless the nighttime routine is complete."

He stood behind her, gently kneading his fingers into her shoulders and the back of her neck. She couldn't lie. It felt absolutely amazing, causing her to relax the tension in her muscles.

"There. How's that for a start to the evening routine?" he asked.

"So good, I don't want you to stop. But I know you probably have to rise and shine early in the morning. You need to get home and get some rest."

Brody shifted to face her. "I will. But, before I do, can we talk about this evening?"

"Sure, what about it? Dinner was lovely, if that's what you mean."

"I'm glad, but that's not what I'm talking about. I feel like things have been off ever since this morning. Well, if I'm being honest, probably even further back than this morning, but today there was definitely something in the air that wasn't right —"

"Brody," she said, placing her finger on his lip. "Outside of my schedule being wonky, absolutely nothing is wrong. I'm being sincere. And, yes, maybe I was a little spacey at dinner, but I promise you, it's just because I'm tired. We're fine, love. Really."

Mack prayed he didn't hear the fast palpitation of her heartbeat. She prayed he would find her response acceptable... even believable. She also prayed for mental clarity. Something she was going to need now that Ben Rowland was back in their lives.

CHAPTER 4

"Hello?" Mackenzie quickly answered the telephone so the ring wouldn't wake Stephanie.

"Mack, it's me, Ben."

She held her breath, feeling somewhat annoyed that she didn't check her caller ID. The conversation earlier in the day was more than she was ready to digest. All she wanted was to relax in bed with the TV playing until she dozed off to sleep.

He continued. "Don't worry. I'm respecting our agreement to give you a week or so to think things over. I promise I called to talk about something different."

"Well, that's good to know. I already feel like my mind is spinning. Time to think would be very much appreciated."

A moment of silence fell between them before he spoke. "I won't lie. I did call to share something else that's been weighing on my heart. Do you have a few minutes?"

She glanced at her digital clock that read nine-fifteen and then hoisted herself to sit upright against her pillows.

"Ben, I have to tell you. From my perspective, this is all very bizarre to me. Just last year this time I had no idea where you were. Now, you're calling me for midday meetings and on the other end of my telephone line just like it's nothing. I can't help but wonder how I'm really supposed to respond to all this."

"I know." He stuttered. "I know, and I completely understand."

"Do you?"

"Okay, maybe I should be careful with what I say. I can only imagine that this must be difficult, having me back in your life. But, I feel like it's my responsibility to make up for lost time. I want to prove to you that I'm not the same man who walked out six years ago."

He cleared his throat. "There's so much more that you need to know, Mackenzie. So much more that I've refrained from sharing since I first reached out to you in April. I'm not the deadbeat guy that you think I am. I haven't been the stupid Ben Rowland that walked out on you for a long time now."

She stared at the ceiling, noticing a subtle crack settling in. "Ben, I'm not trying to be harsh, but why does it matter what I think about something that happened years ago?"

"Because we have a child together, that's why. What you think means everything to me, and it impacts my future with Stephanie. I've already told you how appreciative I am for allowing us to meet and visit on occasion, but someday I'm going to want more. Is it so wrong to hope that someday my kid could come over and spend more quality time with her dad?"

"No, I guess not," she replied, frowning on her end of the line.

"Look, let me start by saying that I have no intention of overstepping my boundaries. None whatsoever. Instead, I called to tell you about a stack of letters that I've been holding for you and Stephanie. I prayed that one day a moment like this would present itself."

Mackenzie scooted to the edge of the bed. "What letters?"

"While I was on the road traveling, we used to have a little downtime on the bus. After writing my songs, I'd spend time each week writing letters to you and Steph. I guess it was my form of a diary, if you will. Plus, a way to stay connected with you, even though we were miles apart. I wrote enough to fill up a shoebox for each of you, and I'm ready to pass the boxes along, if it's okay."

It felt like a frog was stuck in her throat. "I don't know what to say."

"Say that you'll accept the letters. They're all dated. My hope is that it will give you some insight into my heart. And, that you'll learn to trust my intentions. They're sealed. But, if you're curious as to what I wrote in Stephanie's, I'm happy to give you an overview."

"Yes, please. I'd appreciate it," she said.

"Well, I mainly talked about my experiences on the road. The places I'd seen and the people I'd met. But, I also talked about how much I missed her and how I was traveling, hoping to someday return and provide a better life for you two. In the letters I admit the way I went about it wasn't the best choice."

Mackenzie let out a long sigh. "I don't know, Ben. The last part is a lot to unpack. I don't know if she's ready."

"Mack, respectfully, you don't know if she's ready or if you're ready?"

"Maybe a little of both. Although, ever since the day you walked into the café, I think I've been doing a pretty darn good job at rising to the occasion, if I say so myself."

"Yes, you have."

She mustered up the courage to ask the next question, although not one hundred percent certain she wanted to hear the answer. "What did you write in my letters?"

In a deep and rugged voice he replied, "I apologized to you

a thousand times, realizing that would never be enough. I explained how I ran away like a child out of fear that I'd miss my opportunity to pursue my dreams. All this amid you being supportive. What a fool I was back then. A coward and a fool. I also continued to write about how much I was in love with you. And how that didn't just go away because I left. I missed you, Mack, and yearned for you sometimes to the point of tears. I don't know how many times my buddy Chuck caught me soaking my pillow at night. It just didn't make any sense. But, again, I was too selfish to admit my faults and give up life on the road. There was no one to blame for that level of selfishness but me."

Mackenzie paced around her bedroom trying her best to keep her cool. "Am I really to believe that you cared about our existence, Ben? Perhaps those were tears of guilt, but you yearned for me? Come on, give me a break. If that's the way you really felt, then why didn't you come back when you made it big? Why didn't you try and do something to help us out, huh? It doesn't make any sense."

Ben immediately dove in. "It took me practically six years to get my name on the charts. But, I did come back when I made it, Mackenzie. And even now, my name is still not at the top of the billboards, but they know who I am in Vegas and other well-known arenas. That's why I'm here now. If you think for one minute that I was out there living it up, then you're wrong. We struggled, at times trying to figure out where our next meal was coming from. And, as I told you before, I tried reaching out to you. But you cut off our telephone line. Heck, I even tried calling some of our old neighbors, but they all had the same story, which was you had moved away. Then I even called your family—"

"I know...I know. They wouldn't tell you where I was. And rightfully so because I was angry for what you'd done. I never wanted you to find me, and I didn't want them telling me if you had called. You hurt me, Ben. You hurt me to the core. Lucky for you, Stephanie was too young to understand, and in a lot of ways she still is. But, as for myself, the memories are still very fresh."

"I know they are, Mack. I've been treading ever so carefully since seeing you for the first time in years, respecting the fact that I put you in this predicament. But, you need to know that I'm back here with a purpose, foremost to help take care of my daughter and be involved in her life like a father should. I can balance my responsibilities as a father with my career and I plan to show you how. Also—" His voice trailed off.

She clenched her fists, listening intently on the other end of the line.

"If there's a possibility that I can win your heart again, then I plan on doing that as well. I'm talking full-fledged, having you back in my life, and loving you and supporting you completely... the way you deserve to be loved... the way I always should've loved you before I left." He declared.

"Have you lost your mind? I'm seeing someone, Ben."

"The guy that was with Stephanie in the café a few months back?" he asked.

"That's none of your business."

"Well, if I'm going to be around more often, then it should be. Are you guys married?"

"No."

"Hmm." He grunted.

Mackenzie tried to pretend like she didn't care to have anything to do with Ben personally, and for the most part, she didn't. But was it so wrong to desire an explanation for his actions? To ask all the questions she never had time to ask. And to finally have a chance to put the pieces of the puzzle together after so many years.

"Look, Ben, it's getting late. Steph wanted me to ask if you're free to get together soon. If you can just give me a few dates to choose from and maybe we can meet at the park again," she said.

"Uh, let's see. I have a show on Thursday and Friday evening, but Saturday is wide open."

"Saturday works."

"Great, instead of the park, why don't you let me drive you up to the carnival by the Harbor? They have Ferris wheel rides and fun games. I bet Steph would love to go." He begged.

"Bennn."

"Please?" he asked.

She closed her eyes, imagining what Brody would think. Mack hadn't made a real attempt to involve him in this aspect of their lives, and she really didn't have a good reason for it. Other than they were two men, from two different time periods in her life, and she didn't know if the two could mesh. Or if she could personally handle it. *How ridiculous.*

"Let me think about it. I'll send you a message confirming either way."

"Okay, have a good night. Oh, and, Mack."

"Yes."

"I meant what I said earlier. I meant every bit of it. I don't care how long it takes. My mission is to win you and Stephanie back in my life for good."

∽

The next evening, Mae slid into a booth, making herself comfortable sitting across from Meredith and Edith. Over in the corner of the café, she waved at Agnes who was nestled next to Grant, and one booth over was Ms. Violet who was dining alone.

Mae spoke with confidence. "I guarantee one of you will meet a man of interest tonight. If there's anywhere on the Island to meet him, it's right here at Mack's café." She then tapped the table, beckoning for the ladies to lean in. "Okay, so here's the scoop. Meredith, you should know this given that you've been living here longer than me, but since you never hang out in the café, let me fill you in. The woman sitting by herself goes by the name of Violet. Everyone calls her Ms. Violet, if you want to be politically correct. She's a loner for the most part, unless it's bridge club night. Within the hour, all her buddies from the club will round up the tables to play. They take the game so seriously you'd think their lives depended on it." She laughed.

"That's nice and all, but where are the good-looking men?" Edith asked.

"Yeah." Meredith chimed in.

"Here comes one now. His name is Theodore. He's just as serious about bridge as the rest of them. But when the game is over, he and all the gentlemen like to mingle." Mae smiled.

"I know Theodore from the neighborhood. Edith, I'll stay clear and let you have him. The old goat stirs up way too much trouble at the HOA meetings for me," Meredith said, rolling her eyes.

"Now, now, Meredith. You have to learn to be flexible. You might discover that he's not half bad outside of the meetings. You'll never know these things unless you learn to loosen up a bit."

"Mmm hmm. Look who's talking. Aren't you the same woman who almost overlooked your chance at love with Jonathan?" Meredith grumbled.

"No, I'm not. I wanted to ensure that we weren't going to ruin our friendship. That's very different from what you're doing, which is not giving anyone a chance at all."

Mackenzie approached the table with a notepad in hand, ready to take their order.

"Well, isn't this a pleasant surprise, Mae? How are you, dear?" She smiled.

"I'm well, thank you. I brought my neighbors, Meredith and Edith, with me. Both are excited to try out something from the menu." Then she leaned closer to whisper, "And, perhaps have an opportunity to meet some new friends." She winked.

"Ohh, new friends. I see. Well, you picked the right place. The bridge club plus half of Solomons will squeeze in here tonight. I'll keep my eye out for you, ladies."

Everyone smiled.

"Would anybody like to try tonight's special? We have rockfish on the menu, and I can almost guarantee Chef Harold will grill it to perfection, leaving your tastebuds watering for more," she said.

"Sounds good to me. Please throw in the potato fries and green beans on the side," Edith replied.

Mae agreed. "Add two more orders, one for me and one to go for Jonathan."

"How is Jonathan doing?" Mack asked.

"Oh, he's fine. Probably giving his undivided attention to the baseball game since I'm not there to bug him." She chuckled.

"I'll bet," Mack said, then turned her attention to Meredith.

"I'll just have a cup of chicken noodle soup, please."

Everyone peered over their menus to look at Meredith.

"What? I had a big salad for lunch which spoiled my appetite."

Mae shook her head. "Okay, as long as you remember my advice about learning to live a little. If you know we're going out in advance, have a light lunch so you can enjoy something fun." She encouraged.

Mae thanked Mackenzie for taking their orders and waited for her to walk away.

"Meredith, you have to learn to let your hair down a little. No, I take that back, not just a little, a whole lot. You're wearing your girdle entirely too tight around your waist, my dear."

Edith cracked up, trying her best to cover her mouth.

Mae continued. "Don't look so shocked. You're a beautiful woman, smart, and I believe a good catch, but no one will know these things about you if you don't let your hair down and learn to laugh, try new things on the menu, and heck, just loosen up."

Edith interrupted.

"Ladies, you might want to table this topic for now. Your friend, the bridge club enthusiast, is heading over this way," she said, clenching her teeth as she spoke.

Mae perked up and waved him over, noticing Meredith fidgeting with her napkin.

Meredith wore the perfect shade of rouge lipstick and a floral sundress that highlighted her shape. She really was a beautiful woman, but Mae imagined that her dedication to her deceased husband may have influenced her to live such a secluded life all these years.

"Good evening, ladies," Theodore said, speaking to the entire group, but smiling at Meredith.

"How are you, Theo? Long time no see," Mae replied.

"It has been a while. How's Jonathan doing?"

"He's wonderful. I'll have to tell him you asked about him," she replied. "Have you met Edith? She's new to Solomons Island."

"I don't think we have met," he said, extending his hand across the table. Again, Mae noticed his attention return to Meredith.

"We ought to get together this summer. Maybe have a little friendly neighborhood barbecue."

"That would be nice. Maybe Jonathan and I could host in our backyard. I'll bet Meredith would love to join us. After all, she does live right next door," Mae said, observing Meredith turn three shades of red.

"Yesss, Meredith. It would be nice getting to know you outside of the HOA meetings. It would be a nice change in scenery. I'd like that a lot." He smiled. "By the way, you did a fantastic job at the board elections meeting last week. I liked your no-nonsense approach of keeping everybody in line."

Mae saw a smile emerge with a little batting of the eyelashes. It was completely out of character for Meredith to be shy. She nudged Meredith under the table.

"Thank you, Theodore. I also noticed that you have quite a way about you at the meetings. Perhaps you'll consider taking on the president's role in the near future?" Meredith asked.

"Not a chance. I'm happy to go and speak my piece, but I'll leave that job up to somebody who doesn't mind gaining more grey hair." He chuckled, gripping his belt.

Mae elbowed Edith, hoping she too would notice how Meredith smiled at his jokes.

"Well, my game is about to start in a few minutes," he said, standing idle. Then he redirected his attention toward Meredith for the last time. "I sure hope to see you at the barbecue." He smiled.

Meredith glanced at him and then returned to fidgeting with her napkin. "Just name the date, and I'll be there." She smiled back.

Mae lifted her eyebrows, shocked. *Who was this woman?* When Theodore walked away Mae dialed in with questions.

"What was that all about?" she asked.

"What do you mean?"

"The whole batting your eyes and playing shy act. The Meredith I know is much more of a knock on your door and shove a flyer in your face kind of woman. I'm discovering there's a whole side to you that I've yet to learn." Mae chuckled.

"Oh, Mae."

"It's true. What happened to you steering clear of the guy? Did you say something about him stirring up too much trouble at the meetings?" Mae asked, causing her and Edith to laugh even harder.

"Well, that was before I knew he was interested. Did you see the way he looked at me? I didn't realize how cute his smile was before today."

Edith chimed in. "Well, at least one of us is having a successful night. As I look around, I see nothing but a bunch of overly enthusiastic card players. Not exactly my cup of tea. But, I am enjoying the atmosphere, so I'm glad we came just the same. Honestly, tonight serves as a pleasant reminder that I don't necessarily have to have a man to be happy. If I meet someone, then great. But, if not, I can still enjoy my life. The world won't come to an end if I never marry again." She explained.

Mackenzie interrupted, placing their glasses of water at the center of the table. "Ladies, I'm so sorry. It's so busy in here that I failed to ask what you'd like to drink."

"The water is fine for me," Edith replied.

"I'll take a diet ginger ale," Mae replied, and Meredith ordered her usual hot tea.

"Perfect. Your food will be right up," she said, and then slipped a white piece of paper across the table.

"Meredith, this is for you. Theodore asked me to pass it along." Mack smiled.

All the women watched Meredith open the piece of paper. "It's his telephone number," she said. Then they looked over at Theo who smiled graciously at Meredith.

"It's funny how I never detected any interest from him before now," Meredith said.

"Perhaps you didn't want to notice. There's a season for everything, you know," Mae replied.

"Okay, Mae. I get the message loud and clear. Enough about me, what about Edith?"

As Mae sat listening to the banter, she was reminded of how the flames of love were ignited between her and Jonathan. If it wasn't for his persistent pursuit of her affection, she too would have missed her opportunity at love again.

Edith took a sip of the beverage Mack had delivered to the table. "What about me? Are you curious to know how I landed in a state of being all alone and moving to the Island by myself? I'll tell you how it happened. It's the classic tale of a woman who was married to a successful celebrity sports doctor."

Meredith interrupted. "A celebrity sports doctor? That sounds like something out of a Hollywood movie if you ask me."

Edith agreed. "Ha, and I was gullible enough to think the same toward the beginning of our union. I boasted about his career to my folks and looked at him in total admiration in the beginning. I even supported him throughout his career, helping him in every way I possibly could. We never had kids together. I found out I wasn't able to have children very early on. But it didn't matter. We made up our minds to live out our happily ever after... just the two of us. That is, until he decided I wasn't enough for him."

"No way. What did he do, cheat on you?" Mae asked.

"Yep, I guess the exposure to the celebrities who lived the fast life was more than he could handle, causing him to give into the pressure and have an affair. Several of them to be specific." Edith explained.

Meredith straightened her posture, appearing to be rather

annoyed. "I don't get it. Are you trying to suggest that he had affairs with his patients?" she asked.

"No. He ran an ethical practice. That much I'm sure of. But, all the countless parties, and galas, and trips to exotic places. That kind of exposure did him in. Which, in turn, did our marriage in."

"Ohhh, I see. Well, good for you for not tolerating the disrespect. You packed your bags and started a new life on your own. That's to be commended," Mae said.

"Thank you, although I can't sit here and pretend like I don't miss certain aspects of my old life. I miss being cared for. I miss having the companionship in my life. Believe it or not whenever he was home, he was still good to me. But I suppose that's because he figured he could have his cake and eat it too. I know it sounds pathetic, but I miss having a man around to look after me and to help out with simple things like fixing the stupid dishwasher." Meredith complained.

Mae groaned, knowing all too well what she meant.

"Mae Middleton, I owe you an apology." Edith offered.

"What would make you say such a thing?"

"I took advantage of Jonathan's kindness when I first arrived. It's one thing to ask a neighbor for a favor every now and again, but I should've been quicker to find help on my own." She confessed.

Mae was a little surprised to hear her say the words, confirming everything she'd ever thought about Edith in the past. But she'd put all that behind her and was willing to be friends.

"Edith, that's what neighbors are for... but I'm glad you managed to find your own handyman. What's his name again?" She winked.

"It's Timothy from Lighthouse Tours. He's amazing.

Apparently, he does a little moonlighting work on the side. He comes out anytime my machinery needs a little tune up."

"Ha, I'll bet he does." Meredith chuckled.

Just then Mackenzie arrived to serve their meals. The quality time spent at the café was welcomed and much needed by all, perhaps even a new tradition that Mae would actually enjoy.

CHAPTER 5

Mackenzie leaned on the railing of the dock, talking out loud to herself. "I'm not cut out for this." She groaned, wishing she could scream it across the Patuxent River.

She didn't realize she had company, listening to her utter every word until Agnes tapped her on the shoulder. "Having a rough day at the café?" she asked, startling the daylights out of Mack.

"Agnes, I didn't see you standing there. No... everything is fine at the café. Dakota and Joshua have everything covered. I just needed to step outside for a few minutes and get some fresh air."

"Grant and I noticed you rushing out, which is normally so unlike you. I thought I'd come out to see if everything was okay," she replied.

"Everything is fine. Or at least it will be. Just dealing with a few things, that's all. What about you? I see you've been spending a lot of quality time with Grant. How are things going between you two?" she asked.

"Nice deflection, but I'm going to circle back to you after answering your question. Things are going pretty well. He's settled into the beach house and loving it, and so far, he's been quite the gentleman, courting me and being very attentive."

"Whoa, did I hear you use the words courting and attentive in the same sentence? This guy sounds pretty promising," Mack said, trying to muster up an encouraging smile.

"He does. Of course, I tell Clara all the time that I don't want to get too far ahead of myself. I'm just trying to enjoy the ride."

"Has she met him yet?" Mack asked.

"Mike and Clara invited him over for dinner, so far giving him the stamp of approval. But, again, you know my prior history, so one day at a time. Now, enough about me. What would cause Mackenzie Rowland to run outside during the busiest hours of the evening and say, and I quote, 'I'm not cut out for this?' What's going on?"

Mackenzie allowed her head to drop, trying her best to clear her mind.

"Nothing that I can dive too deep into now, but let's just say that my child's father is back in our lives, making decisions that are leaving me between a rock and a hard place. My mind is in a fog as I try to sort everything out, and if I'm not careful, eventually some of this is going to start impacting my relationship with Brody."

"Did he say that?"

"No. Not really. But, it doesn't take a rocket scientist to see that Ben's presence is already starting to take a toll. Thankfully, the only one who's truly happy is Stephanie. I can't blame her for any level of joy that she expresses over Ben's return. All she wants is a relationship with her father, which is to be expected."

Without making eye contact, Mackenzie could feel the presence of Agnes leaning beside her on the dock.

"You know, there's something about this location that brings out the best in people. Maybe it's the soothing sound of the water or watching the boats as they pass by. Maybe it's watching the lovers walk hand-in-hand, right here under the stars. I'm not sure what it is. But, whenever I come out to the dock for quiet walks and to gain mental clarity, it all comes down to one thing. Am I really being honest with myself? That's the question I always have to ask."

Mack drew her eyebrows together like an accordion. "I'm not sure that I follow. I'm doing the best that I can to ensure that through all this Stephanie remains happy and emotionally sound. But my reality is quite different from hers. Ben is not only her father, but before he walked out on us, he was my lover and closest friend. It took me years to get past the idea that he wasn't coming back. And, now that he's here —"

She wiped the moisture away from her eyes and continued staring off into the distance.

"Now that he's here it's doing a number on your heart." Agnes implied.

"No! I mean, I don't know. I'm confused. I want to be one hundred percent angry with him, but if I go around holding such animosity, then what? It will impact Stephanie. So, I try to lighten up a little. But he's saying and trying to make decisions that are messing with my head. Sometimes, I don't know if I should believe him at all. Other times, when I look into his eyes, I see the old Ben that I trusted, and it makes me question everything."

Again, she smeared a teardrop away from her face.

"What does Brody have to say about all this?"

"He doesn't know. I guess that's another fail on my part,

but why drag him in the middle of all this? At least not until I figure out which way is up," Mack replied.

"I do recall you saying that Ben's presence is starting to have an impact. And, from everything I've learned about Brody so far, he's pretty intuitive. Just be careful. You wouldn't want to make a decision that later on down the line you'll regret. Trust me when I say, I've been there and done that. Picking up the pieces after the fact is no fun."

"Thanks, Ag. If you wouldn't mind, I'd like to keep this between us. There's no point in stirring things up with Brody. He's a good man. He's already had his heart broken once. I want to be really careful with how I proceed."

"Agreed. As far as I'm concerned, we didn't even have this conversation. I won't even say anything to my sister unless you initiate the conversation. But please know that I'm here if you need anyone to talk to." Agnes offered.

"Thanks, love."

Agnes rested her hand on Mackenzie's shoulder before returning to the café. She also needed to get back. But first, Mack closed her eyes quietly, listening to the tranquility of the water. Then she imagined the moment, years ago, when she told Ben they were expecting. All the passion and love between them had produced a child. Something she was elated to announce. The way he placed his hand on her stomach, holding her through the night. All those memories that were buried over the years were resurfacing, playing mind games and toying with her emotions.

Then there was Brody. He'd ignited a flame in her that she didn't realize existed. He was a good guy, wholesome in every way, and loved her daughter like she was his very own. Mackenzie's only dilemma boiled down to one thing — a request made by Ben for her to consider. The same request that, so far, she harbored on the inside and kept as a secret.

"Hey, Mack. Did I catch you at a bad time?" Clara asked.

"No, your timing couldn't be better. I was just closing up the café so I could head home to relieve Stephanie's babysitter. What's up?"

"I hate to be the bearer of bad news, but we just received a phone call from the county police. Brody was rear-ended by a truck. The officer said that the ambulance is taking him to Solomons Hospital. He said they found one of our business cards in his wallet."

"Oh, no. This is terrible. Is he going to be okay?" she asked.

"The officer said by a miracle he doesn't appear to have any broken bones, but he does have a couple of cuts from shattered glass and some bruising. He reiterated that was based on an external observation. Taking him to the ER was the safest bet. The good news is he was totally conscious."

"Man, I need to get over there and see how he's doing. Clara, thank you for calling me. I need to reach out to my sitter and see if she can stay a while longer." She explained.

"No problem. Mike and I are heading over if you'd like to ride with us."

"You guys go ahead. I'll probably need to make a bee-line home after visiting with him. Taking two cars will probably be much easier for both of us, but I'll see you there, love."

Mackenzie slid her hand alongside Brody's cheek, gingerly avoiding his bandages and bruise marks on his face. She glanced over his body, noticing he was covered in a hospital gown with a few cuts and a splint on his finger.

"Oh, Brody," she whispered.

His eyelids opened, looking somewhat tired but alert.

"Mack, what are you doing here?" he asked in a raspy voice.

"I came here to see you. Clara and Mike are waiting in the lobby. I think the real question is what are you doing here? What's this I hear about you getting into an accident? You're one of the most careful drivers I know. And you drive one heck of a pickup truck, made by one of the industry's best. Are you okay?"

He smiled, then coughed and grabbed his rib cage.

"Do you want some of the water the nurse brought in a pitcher for you?"

"No, thank you. According to the doctor I managed to walk away with a broken finger and a concussion. Seems almost hard to believe since my body feels like it's been in a train wreck. I barely recall much since I arrived here. Nothing but a lot of noise and tons of lights. They even laid me down and put me in a machine that banged and knocked so much, it darn near gave me a headache. All that, and now they expect me to rest. Yeah, right." He complained.

"I'm so sorry, Brody. Even though it makes me feel better to know that they've examined you, do you know what caused the accident?"

"No. All I remember is being slammed into and pushed across an intersection. The doctor says my airbag didn't deploy. Guess I was rather lucky," he said, attempting to shrug his shoulders, then shrieking from the pain.

Mackenzie watched as he attempted to sit upright, but that also was a bad idea.

"Brody, I don't think you should try to do anything but rest. From the looks of things, you may experience some discomfort for a while."

"Nah, don't let the bruises scare you. I've been knocked

and bumped around a time or two in my life. This is nothing," he said.

"Hmm, I'll bet if your father knew you were here, he wouldn't say the same. Speaking of which. You'll have to give me his number so I can make him aware."

Brody placed his good finger over her lips. "Shh, you'll do no such thing. My father is probably resting peacefully in Annapolis without a care in the world. The last thing I want you to do is upset him. I'll give him a call when I get out of here, I promise."

"Brodyyy, I don't think that's a good idea. He's your next of kin and should know about your medical condition. As a matter of fact, his number should've been in your wallet. Not just Lighthouse Tours," she said, scolding him.

A lazy smile emerged across his face. "What about your number?"

"What do you mean?"

"They asked if I had someone to call at home. Immediately, I thought of you. Of course, I didn't give them your number because I didn't want to frighten you. It just goes to show, even in a state of confusion, you're still always on my mind."

Mack observed Brody speaking to her with his eyes closed and his hand resting on hers. "Brody, now that I think of it, if you have a concussion, I highly doubt they want you going to sleep."

A nurse came over, interrupting Mackenzie's train of thought. "You're exactly right, ma'am. The doc asked me to keep a close eye on this handsome fella, and I plan on doing just that. You must be the lucky girlfriend that he was telling us about. How are you?" she asked.

"I'm well, thank you. But I'm mainly concerned about Brody. Is he going to be okay?" Mack asked.

"Oh, he's going to be just fine. You have one tough cookie

on your hands. He has a few bumps and bruises, a broken finger, and he banged his forehead and the steering wheel pretty badly. He'll need to stay here for a twenty-four-hour observation, but as long as everything else continues to go well, he can be released tomorrow. Is it all right to assume that you'll be here to give him a ride home?"

"Yes, of course."

The nurse patted Mack on the shoulder. "Very well. The doctor will start making his rounds within the next half hour. I'll let you two visit until the thirty minutes are up."

"Ma'am, Brody's boss and his wife are waiting in the hall. Can they come in to see him as well?"

The nurse tilted her head toward Mackenzie, raising her hand to her hip. "Sorry, the ER only allows one visitor at a time. The best I can do is allow you ten minutes and then you can switch. I'll go let them know if you'd like," she said.

"I'd appreciate it. They're both standing just outside the double doors in the hall."

"Mmm hmm."

Mack watched as she walked away, noticing her mock scrub dress with opaque stockings and thick clogs. She was old-fashioned, somewhat stern if she was being honest, and wore a uniform that looked like it was straight from the eighties. But, more importantly, she was looking after Brody, and that's all that truly mattered.

Brody rubbed his finger across her hand. "She's an authoritarian for sure, but don't let that fool you. She and the team of nurses on shift are taking good care of me. As soon as they wheeled me in here, she barked a few orders and they had me in the back for testing in no time."

"Well, that's good to hear. How's your head feeling?" she asked.

"Like it's been in an accident with a Mack truck, but that's to be expected." Brody tried chuckling and making light of it, but it wasn't going over so well.

"Hey, Mack."

"Yes?"

"Before you leave, there's something I've been meaning to ask you."

"Sure, love. Do you need me to bring you something from your place so you can be comfortable here tonight?"

"No. Although I appreciate it, the only place I want to get comfortable is at home. They're giving me some of the basic necessities. The rest I can take care of when I get home tomorrow," he replied.

"Okay, well, in that case what do you need?"

"I need you to level up with me. Things have been a little different with us as of late. I could go out on a limb and say things started getting a little awkward not long after Ben showed up. Is there something you want to tell me?" he asked in a low, raspy voice.

Mack swallowed as she tried to think of a way to properly respond.

"Brody, now is the time to focus on you. You're lying in a hospital bed, thankfully still in one piece after being in a terrible car accident." She emphasized, placing her hand on his arm.

"Please, don't do the whole avoidance thing. I know where I am, and I definitely know why I'm here. But the only thing on my mind right now is ensuring all is well between us. If there's something I need to know, I'd much rather you come out and tell me."

She withdrew her hand but still continued offering words of comfort. "I guess I owe you an apology. I'll admit that I'm still trying to sift through a lot right now. Figuring out what kind of a father Ben is going to be in Stephanie's life, and how often he should see her, and on and on...it's a lot, Brody. But, in no way do I want that to interfere with us."

She watched as he rested his head on the pillow.

Brody continued. "That brings me comfort. When I get out of here and get myself together, I hope you'll consider introducing me to him."

"Brody, I don't know —"

"Hold on. I just asked you to consider it. You don't have to respond now. Just consider it," he said, this time sharing another lazy smile.

"I will."

Mack moved closer to his side of the bed, finding just the right spot near his temple to give him a gentle kiss. "I better make sure I follow the nurse's orders. Heaven forbid I cause her to tower over us again with her hands on her hip." She teased.

"Ha, that's right. Heaven forbid. I love you, Mack. Thanks for coming here tonight."

Mackenzie cracked a smile. "Are you kidding me? If it weren't for the strict rules here in the ER, I'd stay even longer. Don't you worry. I'll be back tomorrow so that I can escort you home. I'll go talk to the doctors now to see what time is best to be back here tomorrow."

She kissed his hand, then tucked it over the covers before walking out to the main lobby. On her way out, guilt washed over her, knowing she had way more on her mind than she originally let on.

∾

Mae and Jonathan glanced over at their sailing partners for the afternoon. With the warm sun beaming on their skin and the wind flowing through their hair, Theodore and Meredith appeared to be getting along quite nicely, enjoying each other's company on their ride to Annapolis.

Mae whispered to Jonathan, "You know, there's something about sailing and falling in love that goes hand in hand." She winked.

"Really? Please elaborate. I'd be very interested in hearing the connection," Jonathan said, somewhat mocking her.

"It's rather simple. Both sailing and falling in love allow you to feel free." She explained, closing her eyes and inhaling.

"Good grief." He smiled.

"Jonathan, you're just jealous of my matchmaking skills. I can't help that I'm a natural. Just look. It's a gorgeous afternoon. We're out here on the water, and we're not the only ones having a good time." Mae winked at the happy pair sitting along the side of the boat.

Meredith and Theodore engaged in light banter back and forth.

"Mae and Jonathan, this is way better than our original plans for a backyard barbecue. Don't get me wrong. I love a good cookout, but you can't beat this view. Now I see why you were so excited to purchase a boat. This is amazing, isn't it Theodore?" Meredith asked.

Mae nudged Jonathan, feeling even better about her matchmaking efforts. "If you think this is nice, you'll have to make it down to the Carolinas with us some day. Isn't that right, honey?" she asked Jonathan.

"Yep." He nodded along, giving her a little smirk.

Mae knew exactly what he was thinking. Jonathan probably assumed this whole matchmaking thing was going to her head.

Mae continued. "Jonathan and I sailed with the grandkids over their spring break. It was such a wonderful trip." She grabbed him by the hand.

"It was. The next trip we hope to plan for is Tybee Island in Georgia. Although, I've heard a lot of nice things about the Bahamas as well," Jonathan said.

Theodore's eyes widened. "And here I thought I was living a good life. You two are giving a whole new meaning to traveling in style." He joked.

Mae noticed Meredith soaking up every word Theodore spoke. She thought it was sweet and was happy to see her relaxing and having a good time. Clearly, any past issues she'd had with him were behind her.

"It's too bad we couldn't convince Edith to come along. I think she would've enjoyed herself," Mae said.

Theodore crinkled his eyebrows. "Is that the new neighbor you introduced me to?"

"Yes, that's her. She's divorced and we were thinking it might be nice for her to meet a new friend. Do you have any bachelor friends we could introduce her to?"

Jonathan shook his head. "Mae Middleton, how do you know that Edith wants you scouting around for a male companion on her behalf? Do you really think that's a good idea?"

"I was just subtly asking if he knew of anyone. There's no harm in helping two single people wind up in the same place together. Anything that happens after that is on them." Mae reasoned.

"Is that how it goes? Interesting. And did I hear you use the word subtle? There's nothing subtle about your approach, Mae. Absolutely nothing at all." He laughed.

She waved him off, thinking nothing of her innocent gesture, when her cell phone rang.

"Excuse me, it's our boss Mike. He rarely disturbs us on a day off unless it's something important. I need to take this call."

Mae explained, stepping to the back, swiping the screen to accept the call.

"Go right ahead. We'll be here when you get back," Meredith said.

"Hello, Mike?"

"Do you have a minute?" he asked.

She plugged her other ear trying her best to hear him against the force of the wind. "Yes, but I can't guarantee the connection won't be dropped. I'm on the water with Jonathan and a couple of friends. What's wrong? You sound upset."

"Upset would be an understatement, Mae. I'm trying to figure out what's going on. In all your years of working with us, you're usually pretty careful when helping out with orders. You normally check with Clara and myself if you have any questions. But this time we have a huge invoice with your signature written all over it and stacks of boxes in the back that cannot be explained," he said.

"Oh, you must be referring to the parts for our rental equipment. Yep, that was me. I placed the order all right. But I was only following up with the reminder Clara placed in the computer."

"What reminder, Mae?"

"I read it verbatim. It said place order for parts today. It popped up in big bright red letters, and I specifically remember it was the weekend I covered the office while you and Clara went to visit your parents. I've placed orders before while covering the front desk. I don't see what the problem is," she replied, feeling herself getting a little overheated.

"Mae, you've placed orders for us before, but it was always specific orders by request, under my direction. When I arrived here today, there were boxes upon boxes stacked a mile high with boating and rental equipment with a final invoice in the thousands. The reminder you saw on Clara's computer was for a much smaller order," Mike said.

"I know for certain there was an order that was drafted and ready to go in the system, Mike. I have no reason to make this up."

She could hear him sigh on the other end of the line.

"Yes, but that order was exactly as you said, a draft. An ongoing draft that wasn't going to be submitted until the beginning of the new year. We planned to revise it and tweak it to make it align with our needs for the new year. To make matters worse, this shipment can't be returned."

"Oh, no."

"Right. The order should've never been placed, signed for, or accepted." He explained, sounding more serious than she had ever heard over their years of working together.

Mae stood watching Jonathan steering the boat, and Meredith and Theodore laughing with one another while in the pit of her stomach she literally felt sick.

"Mike, I'm so sorry. I had no idea."

"My point exactly. This order is going to create a setback in the budget. The only way I can see to resolve this is by—"

Before Mike could finish, the call dropped, leaving Mae with a sick feeling in her stomach.

CHAPTER 6

Mackenzie drew the covers up to Stephanie's shoulders while sitting on the edge of her bed.

"Is Brody okay?" Stephanie asked, half awake and very groggy.

"He's going to be just fine, love. What are you still doing up?"

"I was worried about Brody. Annie told me that you had to go to the hospital to see him."

Mack brushed her hair to the side. "Well, I promise there's nothing for you to worry about. The doctor just wants to watch Brody overnight, and then I will go pick him up tomorrow. Staying overnight is just a precaution."

"A precaution?" Steph asked, fumbling over the pronunciation.

"Yes, just to be safe because he hit his head. The one thing I know for certain, if Brody were here right now, he'd want you to go to sleep. He'd be very sad if he knew you were losing sleep over this."

"Okay, Mom. But one more thing. Did you ask dad if we

can do something fun this weekend? I was thinking maybe we could all go fishing, or take him to the Cliffs and hunt for a sabertooth from a shark. Wouldn't that be cool? Maybe Brody can come with us if he's feeling better?" Stephanie begged.

Mackenzie sighed, thinking it was just like a child to see such innocence in everything. Not the least bit concerned of how awkward it may be to have the two men together, one from her past and the other from the present. At least for her it wouldn't be.

"Mommy is so sorry. I forgot to tell you that your dad invited us to go to the carnival up at the harbor this weekend. How does that sound to you?" she asked.

"That sounds fun."

"Good, as for Brody, he's going to need time to heal. Okay, baby?"

"Okayyy," Steph said, closing her eyelids.

Mackenzie planted a soft kiss on her forehead and turned out her lamp. "Get some rest, love. Night night."

"Night, Mom."

On the way to her bedroom, Mack scrolled through three text messages from Ben. All of them showed listings for various properties on Solomons Island, but the last one pleaded with her to call him when she had a chance.

"Mackenzie, keep an open mind for Stephanie's sake," she said out loud. Then she closed her bedroom door behind her.

"Hello?" Ben answered.

"It's me. Hope I'm not calling you back too late."

"No, it's perfect timing. I just got in from band rehearsal. How are you?" he asked.

"I'm exhausted. It's been a very long day and I can't say that I have a lot of energy left in me. However, you asked me to call, so here I am."

"Thank you. I don't intend on keeping you long, but I really need to circle back to the discussion we were having when we met the other day. My hotel fees are already starting to stack up higher than I'd like. Living out of a penthouse suite is nice, but it doesn't quite compare to having a place of my own. I'd love nothing more than to purchase a house and be in close proximity to you and Stephanie." He explained.

"Ben—"

"Hold on, I already know what you're going to say. But please, McKenzie, I need to think about my daughter and making up for lost time with her. My realtor is ready to show me the listings I sent you, but I will only do this if I have your blessing. What do you say, Mack? How do you feel about me moving to Solomons Island and calling it home when I'm not on the road?"

Mack flopped backward on her bed, staring straight up at the ceiling. Somehow this all felt like a crazy dream, except no one was tapping her on the shoulder, trying to wake her up. In fact, nobody knew. Not her best friend, Clara, or her loving companion, Brody. Up until now, the fact that Ben wanted to move to the Island had been her own little secret.

"What can I say, Ben? Who am I to stand in the way of rebuilding a relationship with Stephanie? Who am I to tell you where you can and can't live?" She sighed.

Ben let out a joyous yelp, followed by laughter. "Does this mean you're giving me the okay? I can really go ahead and see a few places on Saturday morning and Sunday if needed?" he asked.

"Again, who am I to stand in the way? I should caution you to think long and hard about the impact this decision will have on Stephanie. If you do this, you need to be committed."

"I would think the impact would be a positive one, I hope."

"Well, Solomons Island is a small place with families who've lived here for generations. Everyone knows each other out here. If you make one poor decision, like fleeing out of Steph's life again, it will have a tremendous effect on her heart and her social life. She's already been teased for not having her dad around before. All I'm asking is that you think long and hard about what you're doing. There's plenty of towns to settle in somewhere between the Harbor and Solomons Island, you know."

"Mackenzie Rowland, I get that you're still afraid. My track record is nowhere near clean. But the fact that I'm willing to plant roots and put my name on a deed to be closer to her should speak volumes about my intentions." He explained.

"Intentions. Mmm. Well, all I can do is pray for the best to come of this situation and ask you to make your daughter proud."

He replied, "And you, hopefully?"

"Mmm. I think you should just worry about Stephanie, for now. Speaking of Steph, she's excited about going to the carnival on Saturday. What time would you like for us to meet you?"

"I'll be in the area. I'll pick you guys up around noon," he said.

"Ben, that doesn't make sense. When we're done at the carnival, you'll still have to drive over an hour to get back to Solomons."

"Perfect. More quality time with my girl. I'll see you at noon?" he asked.

She exhaled. "Okayyy, if you insist."

When the call ended, she mashed a pillow over her head, disgusted at herself for not being more assertive. Although, she could never really tell him where he could and couldn't live. So, instead, she groaned and buried her head underneath the pillow.

"We need to talk." Mack conveyed as she and Clara took an early morning stroll across the beach.

Taking the day off was a no brainer. She'd dropped Stephanie off at day camp and was scheduled to pick up Brody in a few hours, but for now, what Mack needed most was to finally confide in a friend.

"I'm just glad to hear you admit it. I feel like you've been in hiding as of late. What's going on, Mack? Are things alright at the café?" Clara asked.

"Why does everyone assume that whenever I'm stressed it has to do with the café?" She chuckled.

"Well, I don't know. You just recovered from a major fire in the spring. That in itself could've been life altering," Clara replied.

"Yes, but thankfully, we recovered nicely. I still have a way to go before paying off the place, but the café is going to be okay."

Clara stopped and watched as Mack closed her eyes, taking in the morning breeze.

"Then my only other guess has to be a matter of the heart," she said.

"Now we're talking."

"Oh, Mack. I'm sorry. Is it Ben? Is he getting in the way of things between you and Brody?"

"How did you know?" Mackenzie asked.

"I didn't, but apparently Brody had a man to man with Mike. Please don't say anything, but Mike said he seemed real torn up about it."

Mack drew her fingers to her temples, massaging them, trying anything to keep herself calm.

"That's just it. I don't want Brody to have to suffer and go through anything, not on my account. He's been nothing but good to me and Stephanie, and he doesn't deserve to have to worry about me and whether I'm having a change of heart."

Clara put her hand out. "Are you?"

"No. I don't know… or at least I don't think so, but I'm not going to lie, Clara, sometimes I feel confused. I've been going through the motions for Stephanie, trying to do the right thing, but I have to be honest. It's not easy for me. When Ben first re-emerged into our lives, it was strictly business with him, coordinating times where they could talk, then escalating to arranging play dates. But this — nobody equipped me to know how to respond emotionally to being around my child's father and my former lover." She admitted, sounding frustrated.

"Mack, I'm sorry."

"There's no need to be. This is no one's fault but my own. I'm the only one who's in control of my foolish emotions. I really need to get my act together."

"Have you mentioned any of this to Brody?" Clara asked.

"No, but he's very discerning. Clearly, he's been talking to Mike. Plus, even while lying on his hospital bed, he begged me to come clean with him. The only problem is, I don't know what to say. I'm still angry at Ben for leaving us. There's no question, his actions were wrong. But, Clara, when I hear him explain the countless times he tried reaching out to my family and calling the neighbors —"

"Wait. He called your family?"

"Yes. But I'd already asked them to never, under any circumstances, relay the message to me. In my eyes back then, if he had the audacity to walk out, he didn't deserve to be a part of our lives." She explained, drawing lines in the sand with her toes.

"Mackenzie, this is a lot to take in, I understand. But I can't help but wonder, if you thought he wasn't deserving back then, why would he be deserving now?"

"I don't know, people change. And there is a huge part of my heart that is hopeful for Stephanie's sake. I don't remember if I shared with you, but the kids were teasing her at school because her dad was never around for all the activities like the other dads were. Do you know how hard that is on a little girl?" She sighed.

"Makes sense. So, the real aim here is to allow room for their relationship to grow, while not allowing yourself to —"

Mack knew exactly how to finish her sentence. In that moment she could identify exactly what she'd been struggling with up to this point.

"Not allow myself to dwell on the love we had. To leave it in the past no matter how many letters he's written and no matter how many times he tells me that he still wants me in his life."

"What? Wait. Whoa, whoa, whoa. You've been holding out on me." Clara smiled.

"I guess I have. But I swear it's only because my head is spinning, leaving me in a state of confusion. Not because anything happened between us, because it hasn't. Clara, you have to swear to me you will not repeat this to Mike. I want to figure out how to proceed in my own time, and whatever is to come of it, Brody needs to hear it from me." Mack begged.

Clara raised her hands up. "Are you kidding me? I don't want to get caught in the middle of this one. No one will hear a peep from me except you."

"Me?" she asked.

"Yes, you heard me correctly. As your best friend, I need to ask if you've lost your mind? Brody treats you like a queen. He worships the ground you walk on."

Mackenzie continued walking forward, wishing she could make all of it go away, the same way it appeared.

"Yes, he does treat me like a queen, and I love him for it. Honestly, I don't even know why I'm allowing Ben to mess with my head like this. We've been over for such a long time, none of it should matter. But sometimes I wonder about all the unfinished business, you know. There were so many questions I never had the chance to ask, and so many thoughts that were left unspoken. And now he has me curious about these letters that he has supposedly written while he was on the road. All of it makes me just want to get inside his head and figure out what the heck he was thinking back then."

"Mack, whether you're curious about what he was thinking back then or what he's thinking now, you have to ask yourself if it's really worth it. Curiosity can kill you if you're not careful. And, I know it sounds dramatic, but you definitely don't want it to kill your relationship with Brody. He's been here the whole time and he's loyal. I'm not trying to get all preachy but take it from one who spent many years with a man who was not loyal. There's a big difference."

"So, what you're saying is, if you were in my shoes, you'd have absolutely nothing to do with him outside of allowing your daughter to see him. Is that it?"

"Well, it doesn't have to be as harsh as it sounds. You can be cordial but clear. Draw the line so he doesn't think he has a chance with you. Let him know that you're with someone."

"I did, but so far, he doesn't seem impressed. As a matter of fact, he's so not impressed that he's planning on buying a house on Solomons Island."

Mack stopped walking the moment she realized that Clara was a few feet behind waiting to grab her attention. "You can't blame him for that decision, Clara. He's a grown man who can do whatever he wants to do."

She waited as her friend joined her, slowly trying to process it all.

"Did you just say that Ben, the rockstar, is going to be living here? On the Island?" Clara asked.

"I told you that Stephanie's dad is moving here. The rest is up for your interpretation."

Clara patted Mack on the back a couple of times. "Good luck with that one, my friend. Good luck with that."

CHAPTER 7

Mae slipped into Mike's office, awaiting his return from the break room. He'd asked her to go in and have a seat, which made her more nervous than she'd been the day prior. But at this point, she figured whatever consequences were coming her way for the shipment debacle, she may as well brace herself and get it over with.

Mike stepped into the room and closed the door behind him.

"Mike, I can understand if you want to fire me. Let's face it, I made a huge mistake. Like... a huge mistake. But I've been talking this over with Jonathan, and I would hope after all my years of service, you would at least allow me to explain," she said, folding her hands together to keep them from feeling shaky.

She watched as Mike relaxed in his chair, taking his first sip of coffee. "I hadn't even said anything yet, Mae, but I would like to hear an explanation. The floor is yours. Walk me through what happened, because I'd really like to know."

Mae cleared her throat. "It's like I was explaining when you called yesterday. I was covering the front desk, just like I normally would whenever you guys need the extra help. You know my area of expertise is normally giving tours, Mike. It's what I do best. But, on this particular weekend, when you and Clara were out of town, and I saw the reminder on the computer, I figured it had to be important. So, I did what I thought was the right thing, which was look up the order and place it, thinking it would help you to stay on track. As Jonathan pointed out, the only thing I didn't consider was calling to double check with you first, or at least remember to mention it upon your return," she said with her head hanging low.

"Mae Middleton, we've been working together a long time. Therefore, you know I like to run a tight ship financially, ensuring that we manage our funds properly so that employees such as yourself and Jonathan can continue to get paid. Now, unfortunately, the dealers and wholesalers we work with don't care that you were trying to be helpful. They want their money, and their no return policy sticks, especially after you accept and sign off on a shipment. This is what the total invoice looks like. How am I supposed to justify that in our books?" he asked, sliding a copy of the invoice across his desk.

Mae gulped at the amount of zeros that followed the original figure. She'd seen the numbers when the order was placed, but now that she knew her boss didn't approve, all she could do was frown.

"Mae, because of you, we have more LED lights, belts, and trim rings than the law should allow. Everything you see in this order was a foreshadow for the upcoming year." He explained.

"Then why would Clara have it on her computer this year? It doesn't make any sense."

"I asked her about it, and she explained that she must've accidentally set the reminder to the wrong year. Either way, I think it's safe to say that you should've still checked with her. If you did, this whole thing could've been avoided," he said.

"Agreed. I'm sorry, Mike. If you want, you can deduct the amount of money from of my paycheck, from now until I retire. It will probably take that long to pay it back." She teased. Except Mike didn't appear to find it funny. So, she continued. "Or Jonathan and I can come up with a way to pay you back sooner. The call is yours."

Mike reached across the desk, retrieving the invoice. "Thankfully, after careful consideration, I've decided to take the hit on this year's budget, which will leave us with a surplus for next year, given that we'll have all the parts and won't need to place the order. You won't need to pay anything back, and your paychecks will continue as usual. However, Mae. I'm more concerned about the big picture. What would be your takeaway from all this?"

Mae leaned back in her chair, breathing a sigh of relief and rubbing her right temple. "I need to do a much better job at allowing you and Clara to be in charge. After all, you two own the place, not me. I'm just a tour guide, and at times I assist at the front desk. But, no matter which way you slice it, you're still the boss," she said.

"Mae, I appreciate your acknowledgment of my position, but all I really want is to ensure something like this doesn't happen again. In all these years, we've always worked together like a family. A true mom and pop operation. And, yes, sometimes I can be a softy with you because you've been around so long —"

"And because I'm your elder." She interrupted, laughing, but it was true.

"Well, I didn't want to put it that way, but it's true," Mike said, chuckling along with her.

Once the laughter settled down, he continued. "Clara suggested once we had a talk, I'd walk away feeling better and she was right. And now that I know I can count on you to check in with me when big matters come up, I actually would like to propose an idea to see how you'd feel about it."

"What is it?" She smiled.

She watched as Mike stood and began his usual pacing when he had something on his mind.

"Since you and Jonathan have been here the longest, I was thinking about giving you two lead positions. Maybe you can also train some of our new hires."

"New hires? People who would come in and eventually take over our positions?" she asked.

"No, Mae. I would never do such a thing. You and Jonathan are part of what makes this place tick the way it does. As a matter of fact, you're also part of the reason why we'll need to bring at least two new employees on board before the end of the summer. Your tours are in such high demand, we'll need more hands on deck to help you, Jonathan, and Tommy."

"That's wonderful! More hands on deck means more flexibility with scheduling, maybe even more days off?" She grinned.

"Well, hold on, now. One step at a time. I have to start the interview process first. But, if you know of any reliable people who are looking for a full-time position, please let them know we're hiring."

Mae got out of the chair and squeezed Mike until he nearly couldn't breathe. "Thank you, Mike. I thought surely you brought me in here to fire me today. Wait till I tell Jonathan that my dreaded pink slip landed us a promotion." She squealed, then quickly pulled away, regaining her composure.

Mike smiled, revealing his dimples. "One more thing before you go," he said.

"Yes?"

"You and Jonathan are coming up on fifteen years of service for the company. The first ten, with the Annapolis office, and these last five years here on Solomons Island. I think that's worth celebrating, don't you?"

Mae giggled. "What did you have in mind?" she asked.

"Oh, no, no. That's for Clara and me to know, and you and Jonathan to find out. Just make sure you guys clear your calendar for two weeks from this Friday."

"But —"

"Mae, you're not allowed to protest. Just clear the calendar for Friday evening, understood?" he said, lowering his head and looking directly at her.

"Understood. Although Jonathan is not going to be happy to hear about you potentially spending money on us. Especially after the big mix-up," she replied.

"Yeah, well, if need be, I'll remind Jonathan who's boss." Mike winked then opened the door to conclude their meeting.

∼

Brody rested his arm around Mackenzie's shoulders as she escorted him to his couch. Once there he eased into a relaxed sitting position, trying to wish away the discomfort and pain.

It felt like his lower back and every part of his body was screaming for relief, but with another hour left until his next dose of medication, all he could do was live with it. "I have to laugh to keep from crying," he said.

"There's nothing funny about getting into an accident, Brody. It's going to take time for your body to get over the shock of being tossed around by a truck. You're lucky it wasn't worse."

"Agreed. But to think I was doing all the right things, and it still didn't save me from getting into a nasty wreck. It's just a reminder of how short life is. I didn't have to come out of it alive, and I definitely don't take that for granted."

He watched as Mack propped his feet on a pillow and then wedged another one behind his neck.

"Thank you. I really appreciate you being here for me. I realize if it wasn't for me being discharged and needing a ride home, you'd be at the café by now."

"Brody, it's the least I can do. You have me for the whole day until it's time to pick up Stephanie from school. I was thinking about picking up a few groceries for you and preparing a meal that could last you for a few days. By the way, I told her not to worry, but Stephanie was asking about you. She was very concerned when she heard you'd been in an accident," she said.

He patted the empty space next to him on the couch, pleading with her to relax for a moment. "Come sit with me."

The scent of her hair was enough to drive him insane, causing him to temporarily forget about his discomfort. He wanted nothing more than to kiss her but settled for reaching out for her hand.

"Please tell Steph that I'm doing fine. Just a few bruises, that's all. Nothing that won't heal with time."

"I'll tell her, but you know eventually she's going to want to see for herself." Mack chuckled.

"Then bring her over this weekend. I'll certainly be here. It's not like I have a vehicle to drive or anything." As he spoke, pain zipped through his lower back like a flash of lightning, causing him to take a breath.

"Brody?"

"Don't mind me. Keep talking. I've missed snuggling up with you like this. It's been a minute since we just sat down and relaxed together."

"I really think you need to soak in the bathtub while I cook your dinner. Soaking in some warm water and lavender would probably do you a world of good."

Brody drew in a breath and slid his fingers through Mack's. "Listen to me. We have plenty of time for groceries, cooking, and whatever else you have in mind. Heck, I'm easygoing, a pizza pie will suit me just fine. But I need to finish telling you what's been on my mind before it eats me up inside," he said.

"Okay."

"After Mike and Clara left, I laid in the hospital bed, staring at the ceiling, thinking how I was pretty darn lucky to walk away from the accident. The pickup is totaled, literally mangled into pieces, but here I am still alive. Mackenzie, life is way too short to mess around and not go after what you want in life." He explained with a sense of urgency.

"Well, I don't disagree, but I'd also like to think it wasn't your time."

"I'm thankful for that because I have a lot to live for. One of the first things I plan on doing is calling my dad and making arrangements to spend more time with him once I get better." He grunted. "After all, the man only lives an hour away from here. There's no excuse not to see him more often."

"That's sounds wonderful. More time with your father. Check," she said, drawing an imaginary check mark in the air.

"Then there's this other matter I need to boldly step forward and deal with."

"What is it?"

Again, he inhaled the scent of her hair and watched as she breathed, causing his heart to beat abnormally. She sat close enough for him to lean over, slowly gliding his lips onto hers. When he was certain she was receptive, he plunged even deeper, kissing her again.

"Brody," she whispered.

He cleared his throat. "I'm sorry. I got a little carried away."

"Don't apologize. I think it's sweet and very romantic."

"Good, then while I still have the courage, you need to hear what I have to say. I'm ready to propose, Mackenzie. I've been trying to tell you in subtle ways, but life's way too short to be subtle. I want to take care of you and Stephanie, to grow old with you, to love you forever. I've been trying the best way I know how to share this with you, but in one form or another, you've brushed it off. At least up until yesterday. Last night, you told me that all was well with us and there's nothing to be concerned about. If that's really the case, then — marry me," he said, grunting in pain while sliding down to the floor to get on one knee.

"Brody —"

He reached for her hand. "Mack, hold on. Before you say anything, I plan on doing this thing right. I may not have the ring at this moment, but I will have one soon with the biggest diamond I can possibly afford. But, for now, I'm down on my knee as a symbol of my love for you. Please say you'll marry me."

He watched as she appeared speechless, making him even more nervous. "I probably should've had the ring first. You deserve a proper proposal and all… it's just, well, perhaps it's my nerves. It may sound dramatic, but I was lying there in the hospital bed seeing my whole life flash in front me, thinking I'd be a fool if I didn't pour my heart out and claim the woman that I love to be my very own."

Mack positioned herself to face him. "Are you certain you're not just doing this because of Ben?"

He inhaled. "Not sure what would make you think that, but Ben or no Ben, I'm the same man you were talking about building a future with. None of that has changed. At least not on my end."

Brody slowly retracted his hand from hers. "I prayed to God it wasn't true, but the more time that passes, it's clear you're dealing with some sort of internal battle, Mackenzie. One that you need to settle first, before you could ever have this conversation with me."

"No, Brody, I just —"

"We're both adults and we need to be honest here. Things were going very well and now it seems like everything is changing. I have my suspicions, but I won't label it. All I know is I'm in love with you, but I selfishly want you all to myself, not sharing one ounce of your heart with anyone else. So, whatever has been tugging at your heart and mind lately, I want you to go deal with it. Tackle it head on and get it out your system. Perhaps then we can figure out where we really stand."

He slowly hoisted himself back on to the couch, watching as Mackenzie held her head down. "Brody, there's something I need to tell you," she said.

"I'm listening."

It felt like a heavy weight was resting on his chest making it difficult to breathe. But it wasn't like he hadn't been in this position before, on the receiving end of what was about to be bad news. He was a pro at this point, practically bracing himself for the inevitable.

"Ben is looking to buy a house here on Solomons Island so he can be closer to Steph when he's not traveling. He specifically met with me to ask my permission to begin the search process," she admitted.

"Okay, while I'm not sure why he had to meet about it, I guess that's not a terrible thing if the guy plans on playing an active role in her life."

"He definitely wants to play an active role. But there's more. He's in town this weekend and wants to take us to the carnival near the Harbor. It's near the hotel where he has a contract to do a few shows. Stephanie has been so eager to spend time with him, I figured this would be good for them." She explained.

"Okay, I still don't see what the big deal is. All of these things are to be expected when a father is trying to reconnect with his child."

"He also confessed that he tried doing everything he could to find me when he was on the road touring with the band, including reaching out to my folks, but under my direction, they never told me. In addition, he admitted he wrote letters to Stephanie and me over the years, saving them, and I believe he plans to give them to us this weekend. He's been real transparent about his mistakes and about his feelings."

A moment of silence fell between them.

"Oh, I see. Wow. Sounds like you two have had a lot of time to reconnect," he said.

"Brody, I swear there's absolutely nothing going on between us. He's the one that reaches out to me, and to be frank, I'm having a hard time digesting it all. My only fault was keeping everything a secret from you. It's driving a wedge between us, and that's not something I ever wanted."

"I'm not sure why you wouldn't just tell me. Do you have feelings for him?" he asked.

Brody watched as she fiddled nervously with her fingers, recognizing the tell-tale signs of a woman who was having a change of heart. In his eyes, Mackenzie was one of the good ones, so maybe it was something about himself that was off-putting. Or maybe he wasn't assertive enough and clear about his expectations when it came to matters of his own heart. If that was the case, maybe it was high time that he changed.

"Never-mind. There's no need to answer that question." He stood to his feet slowly, straightening up. "As I said earlier, I think you need time to sort things out. Time that doesn't involve me interfering with talks of marriage or anything like it. I've already been down this road before and can recognize when a woman needs her space," he said.

"Brody, I'm not trying to hurt you. Ben's return is still so new. I'm struggling to know which way to turn next, and it feels like everything is spiraling out of control."

"We're not out of control. At least we haven't been up to this point. Either way, I'm stepping aside so you can figure things out without interference," he offered.

"Stepping aside? What does that mean?"

"It means that clearly what I'm currently doing is not working. From the moment I took you on our first date, I knew you were the one. I repeatedly poured out my heart, expressing exactly how I felt about you and Stephanie. I've been there for you and supported you through the most difficult times in your life, but none of that matters anymore. All that matters is Ben is back. He swoops in after years of being M.I.A. and now he has your undivided attention. I can't compete with that. I won't compete with it." He straightened up, winced, and walked to the kitchen.

"Brody, I wish you would sit down and let me whip up something for you. Let me take care of you, that's what I'm here for. And, for the record, I never said you had to compete with Ben." Mack explained.

He stopped in his tracks. "Sadly, you never said anything, Mackenzie. You've been keeping everything to yourself. You haven't even tried to introduce me to the guy, or set any boundaries, letting him know where you stand. And that's fine. We all have different ways of dealing with things, but it's all the more reason why I think you should take as much time as you need to figure this out."

"What about you? What are you going to do here by yourself, with no way of getting around?" she asked.

"Don't worry about me. I'll figure something out." Somehow, after the words were spoken, he knew he meant it in the most literal and figurative way possible. Brody would figure out how to gather the broken pieces of his heart and move forward, even if it meant Mackenzie would no longer be by his side.

CHAPTER 8

Mae reached to cut off the lamp on her nightstand and slid into bed next to Jonathan. "Did you see the way Theodore was all over Meredith on Sunday? It appears as though she liked it. Those two were practically cooing at each other like a couple of teenagers in love. I didn't realize she had it in her." Mae laughed.

"Let them be, Mae. You did your part by introducing them, and you went above and beyond to play matchmaker, but don't you think we ought to stay out of it now? You know, let them have a little space to get to know one another?"

"Oh, they're getting to know one another just fine." She continued, laughing.

Realizing that Jonathan didn't see the humor in it, she moved on. "All right, I'll leave them alone, but one would think you'd at least be proud that I stepped out of my comfort zone and interacted with the neighbors. I spent more time with Edith and Meredith this week than I have with any neighbor since I've been living here."

Mae could feel Jonathan rolling over to spoon with her,

which she loved. It was the only way she'd comfortably fall asleep.

"I'm proud of you. As it turns out, Theodore is a decent guy. After shooting the breeze with him, I wouldn't mind hanging out again. Of course, I'll leave that up to you and Meredith to arrange. On another note, I want to know how things turned out with you and Mike this morning. Of all days for us to have completely different schedules! I've been dying to hear what happened. Whatever you do, please tell me the end result doesn't involve me having to empty out the savings account, does it?" Jonathan asked.

"Not to worry, dear. Everything worked itself out just like I knew it would."

He chuckled. "Mae, please. You're not fooling anybody. You left worried and afraid that Mike was going to give you a pink slip. The conversation must've gone very well for you to be this nonchalant."

Mae swatted at him. She loved Jonathan dearly, but he always had a way of stealing her thunder, bringing her right back down to reality. "He sat me down in his office and explained my error."

"Which was?" Jonathan probed.

"Placing an order without their consent. Any other time it would've been a helpful gesture. I'm certain of it. But this time, Clara was drafting an order and not actually meaning to send it. Either way, I was wrong, so Mike gently scolded me for it."

"That's it? I'm surprised. How much did you say that bill came to again?" he asked.

"An amount so high he had every right to take it out of my paycheck. But he didn't. He said they were going to make adjustments to the budget, balancing everything out, and creating a surplus for next year."

She felt Jonathan's hand slide around her waist, giving her a gentle squeeze.

"Jonathan, I figured you'd be happy to hear the news, but it actually gets better."

"How so?"

"Mike is planning something to celebrate our fifteenth anniversary with the company. Isn't that wonderful?"

"Ordinarily, I would say yes, but given what just happened, I think we need to pass. The last thing I want is Mike to take another hit to his budget," Jonathan said, now adjusting himself to lean upright against his pillow.

Mae knew him like she knew the back of her hand, fully expecting that he would refuse.

They were both stubborn in that sense, but it's part of what attracted to one another.

"I tried to tell him there was no need to make a fuss, but you know Mike. Honestly, I feel pretty honored to have worked for Lighthouse Tours all these years. It's going to be hard parting ways when it's time to retire," she said.

"Agreed. At some point Mike will have to start searching for new blood. Somebody to take over the tours and add their own personal touch to the industry."

"Funny you should mention it because he is already looking to hire some new people. As a matter of fact, you and I are being promoted and will be training the new hires. Can you believe that?" She smiled.

"Uh, no. I can't believe it. We've always been a very small operation. Are you sure he's not trying to replace us now?"

"Nooo. Don't worry, I asked him just to be sure. He says he's ready to expand. The way I look at it, the more the merrier. Maybe that way I can enjoy some time off here and there. Once the trainees get a good handle on things, of course. Then before you know it, five years will be up, and we can spend more time enjoying Solomons and traveling with the grandkids," she said, gliding her feet along his.

"I definitely agree with spending more time with the grands, but I was hoping by then they could come visit us in the south. You know, in a state like Florida, where we can live comfortably and continue sailing as we've always enjoyed."

Mae rose up, also propping herself on a pillow with all thoughts of getting some rest completely exiting her mind.

"With the house being paid for, I don't really see the need to go anywhere. Solomons has suited us just fine since we moved here. No point in upsetting the apple cart now, dear." She suggested.

"I hadn't considered the apple cart, Mae, but I am considering our budget and how much more of an improved lifestyle we would have if we retired south. For one, the taxes are much lower in Florida. Wouldn't you like to live in an area with lower taxes? We will be on a fixed income, you know."

"I understand, but our roots are on the Island. Our doctors, our friends, and our adopted family at Lighthouse Tours. Plus, we're as close as we can possibly get to my daughter, her husband, and the kids. No way could I ever consider moving. It just wouldn't make any sense."

The back of Mae's neck began feeling steamy. Jonathan knew how much she didn't like change. Why he would even consider pressing the matter was beyond her comprehension.

Jonathan continued pressing the matter. "For one, I don't see how you could have such a strong opinion about something you've never explored, Mae. You seem to be so open to visiting new places when we travel on the boat. Why wouldn't you at least visit Florida first and then share your thoughts about it? You might be pleasantly surprised."

"I've been to Florida plenty of times. It's a hot spot for the young and vibrant, and on the flip side it can be wonderful for a retiree... just not this particular retiree. We can go visit these places all you want, Jonathan, but my heart is settled on living and dying right here on the island."

"Mmm, I see. Well, must I remind you that you're not single anymore? Don't you think this is a decision we should make together?" he asked.

"Jonathan, I'm not sure how we started down this road. Retirement isn't for another five years. And, who knows, maybe by then I won't even want to retire. Maybe I'll just continue working to keep myself occupied."

He laughed, which of course only made her blood boil even more.

"So, to make sure I understand you correctly, you would go as far as not retiring just to have your way? Mae, that's just about the most foolish thing I've ever heard. We have so much to look forward to. We bought the boat so we could travel and go on adventures together and enjoy life. Now, the moment I mention something to you about retiring elsewhere, you decide you want to work longer? That doesn't make any sense."

"It may not make any sense to you, Jonathan. But, if extending my time at Lighthouse Tours is what I have to do to ensure —" Her voice trailed off, fully realizing she was allowing her emotions to get the best of her.

"Interesting. You know what? Before either of us says something we may soon regret, perhaps the best thing for me to do is sleep in the guest room tonight. This conversation probably should've ended before now, as far as I'm concerned," he said.

With the moonlight shining in the window, Mae could see the reflection of Jonathan's striped pajamas as he rose out of bed. She looked over, contemplating whether she should speak up. But her stubbornness got in the way, causing her to remain silent while watching him leave.

CHAPTER 9

Mackenzie watched as Ben straddled Stephanie on his shoulders at the carnival. With a teddy bear in hand and a full belly, plus plenty of ice cream, Stephanie was having the time of her life. Mack, on the other hand, struggled to remain in the moment, still feeling burdened by her conversation with Brody.

"Steph, how would you like to spend your last few tickets, baby? Would you like to go on another ride?" she asked.

"No. I think I want to try and win the panda bear, right over here."

"Are you sure? Winning may not be as easy as you think. You have to knock out all the bowling pins at the same time."

"I know," she replied.

Ben placed her down on the ground and passed along the tickets. "You can do anything as long as you put your mind to it, kiddo. Your mother and I will be standing right here, cheering you on." Ben encouraged.

Steph passed her bear over to her dad. "Can you hold this for me?"

"I sure can. Now, go ahead and knock out every pin in sight."

"Maybe you and Mommy should have your cameras ready, just in case I make a strike. You wouldn't want to miss something that big." Steph released her bear, then skipped off, leaving them laughing together.

"Aww, that kid. She's one of a kind." Mack smiled.

"She sure is. You've done a fantastic job raising her. I always knew you were destined to be a good mother."

Mack paused, checking to make sure Steph was good. "Really? How did you know such a thing? I didn't have any experience with kids when we met. All my family lived on the other side of the country, making it difficult to see each other, so what caused you to feel that way?"

He stepped closer. "Are you kidding me? You were nurturing in every way. A woman who has a hot meal prepared when you come home and goes out of her way to take such good care of you... well, I'd like to think if she'd do that for you, then she'd do the same for her child too."

Mack grunted, except she didn't mean for it to slip.

"Did I say the wrong thing?" he asked.

"No."

"Mackenzie, I can see it all over your face. Be honest with me, I can handle it."

She flashed two thumbs up to Steph. "It's okay, love. Give it another try. You can do it!"

Until now, she hadn't considered the attraction that still existed between them, however slight on her part. She'd been too busy hiding behind her frustration since he arrived to give it much thought. But, he was good looking, clean shaven, with muscles and a six-pack that had shown through his shirt. In her opinion, there had to be plenty of women waiting in line to spend time with him.

A serious look stretched across her face. "When you talk about how nurturing I was, I can't help but wonder how you can say that in one and it worked out for you; congrats I'm happy for you you.breath, yet still leave me the way you did. In my mind, it doesn't make any sense."

"I see."

"What exactly do you see, Ben? I'd like to know."

He waved at Steph, giving her an encouraging smile. "I see that you're hurt. And, I take full responsibility for being the one who hurt you. I also see an opportunity to try and make amends. To try and turn the tide if you will let me." He offered, sliding his hand over hers.

She nervously held her breath, allowing her hand to remain in his for what felt like a minute, before pulling away. "I think we should be very careful not to confuse our purpose. The sole reason we are here is Stephanie. As long as we stay focused on Steph, then you and I will be fine." She implied.

He raised both hands. "Okay, I apologize. You're right. Stephanie is the reason why we're here. And, on that note, this is probably a good time to update you on how things went with the house this morning."

"I'm listening."

Ben extended his hand to shake hers. "You are now looking at the proud owner of seventy-five Elderberry Lane," he said with a huge grin smeared across his face.

"You actually bought the house?"

"Yes, and not only that, I worked out a deal to help speed up the closing process. It was a cash deal, so I don't have to wait nearly as long to get in. The family is willing to move within the next two weeks, leaving me with a new place to call my own when I return from Vegas next month."

Mackenzie inched several steps closer to Stephanie's game

to not lose sight of her. "Must be a nice feeling. I guess congratulations are in order."

"Thank you, I was hoping on the way back, we could swing by the street so I can show you and Steph. I figured she'd get a kick out of it. We can't go inside, of course, but maybe a fun drive by. What do you say?"

Feeling reluctant, Mack deflected to Stephanie. "How many tickets do you have left, sweetheart?"

"Twenty," she yelled.

"Oh dear."

"What did you say, Mommy?"

"Nothing, love. I'm right here if you need me," she responded, rocking back and forth from her heels to her toes.

Ben waved his hand in front of Mackenzie. "Hello? I'm still waiting to hear what you think. Come on, aren't you the least bit excited to see it?" he asked.

"Truthfully, I don't know how to feel or what to say, Ben. I'm trying my best to tread lightly here, but you're not making it easy."

"Well then, stop trying to tread and just be truthful with me. Tell me something. Anything is better than nothing," he replied.

"Okay, fine. In my opinion, you're moving way too fast. I can't understand for the life of me why you're always in such a hurry, moving at lightning speed with everything you do. You blasted out of our lives, thrusting yourself into the entertainment business, and it worked out for you, congratulations, I'm happy for you. But now you're back, operating at the same lightning speed, with no regard for whom you may affect along the way. What do you really think you're going to accomplish by moving to the Island? Today you say it's for Stephanie, but tomorrow, you'll be right back on the road, leaving your child with nothing but an empty house to drive by."

"Whoa. Perhaps I hit a sore spot. I can understand you're upset, Mack, but I'm really not the same guy you knew back then. I bought this place because when I'm not doing shows at the Harbor, or on the road—"

He was interrupted by a fan passing by, seeking his autograph. Mack sighed, wishing more than anything that Stephanie would run out of tickets.

Ben signed her t-shirt and then faced Mack and said, "When I'm not working, I plan to be here. This is home base for me now. Something I haven't had in a long time. I don't know that I could ever say anything that will make you feel better, Mackenzie. The only thing I can offer you is time. Time to prove that I'm now a man of his word."

"That's all well and good, but your allegiance needs to be with Stephanie. That girl is going to be through the moon when she finds out you bought a home. She's going to view this as permanent. As in forever. If you don't uphold your promises to her, she will be devastated, Ben. Absolutely devastated."

∼

"Here are the keys. I want you to give your father a kiss and head inside. I'll be right behind you," Mack said.

She watched as Ben bent over, giving Stephanie a kiss. Usually, their departures were met with promises to see each other again soon. A promise she'd always quietly hoped he could keep.

"Bye, Dad."

"See you, sweet girl."

Once Stephanie was out of sight, she noticed Ben walking around to the trunk of the car.

"I have something for you."

"Ben, you didn't have to do that. Taking us to the carnival was more than enough."

He pulled two shoe boxes out of the trunk, then slammed the door down. "As I explained over the phone, I'd been saving these for you and Stephanie. They're letters from my time spent on the road, some written a month apart, some longer than that, but they're all here. I probably should've stored them in a wooden box or something like that, but here they are. All intact."

He placed the boxes on the hood of the car near where she was standing, watching as Mack slid her hand across the lid. "I didn't realize you were much of a writer," she said.

"Neither did I, outside of song writing, of course. But, when you go through a few trials, that's when you start to discover all sorts of things about yourself you didn't realize were true. I wrote about some of those trials in those letters to you, and I wrote about them in my songs."

A slow smile emerged across Mackenzie's face, "You wrote about us in your songs?" Normally, she wasn't impressed with anything having to do with celebrity life. She still wasn't, but to think they were on his mind enough to include them in his music caught her attention.

"I had to make a few name changes and orchestrate the lines to be discrete, but yes, I have a song about daddy's little girl, and another about a long-lost love."

A huge lump began forming in her throat. "Hmm, I didn't realize. Then again, I really don't listen to music much," she said.

"I'll have to get you a copy of my cds. I recorded a lot of life experiences on several tracks."

"Sure." She looked away, knowing if she didn't, she might blush or even reveal too much curiosity about him personally. "By the way, I didn't say anything earlier, but the house looks great. You'll certainly have plenty of yard space. Something that Stephanie was thrilled about as to be expected."

"Yeah, did you see the look on her face when I mentioned the idea of installing a swing set? I'm not going to lie, it felt pretty good seeing her face light up like that. Thank you, Mack, for allowing me to share moments like that with her. It means a lot," he said.

"Mmm hmm." Mack chuckled. "We've been living in this garden apartment ever since I came to the Island," she said, pointing toward the small brick building. "I always wanted to give her more but couldn't afford it. Then came the whole idea of buying the café. I don't expect to ever strike it rich there, but it provides a nice living."

Ben stepped close enough for his cologne to awaken her senses. "You've done an amazing job, creating a happy life for her. Don't ever compare or try to downplay it."

Mackenzie shook the boxes, playfully listening to the sound of letters shifting around. "Well, it looks like you've given us plenty to keep us occupied for the remainder of the summer. I should probably head inside and check on Steph. Thanks again for taking us to the carnival. She had a great time."

"I'm glad. I was hoping you enjoyed yourself as well. I don't know about you, but for me being together, started bringing back old memories." He smiled.

She slowly backed away, waved, then turned around to head inside. "It was a very nice day. Have a good night, Ben."

"Maybe we can talk tomorrow? I'd love to make plans again soon," he called from a distance.

She paused, desiring to seize the opportunity to say what was really on her heart. "Um, yeah. About that, Ben. I think it's best we learn to establish some boundaries. Especially since you're going to be living nearby. I'm okay with you calling to talk to Stephanie. I'm even okay with you texting to make arrangements to spend time with her. But anything outside of that is where I have to draw the line."

"What do you mean?"

She held up the boxes in her hand. "No matter what you've written in these letters, there are simply some things that will never change for me, Ben. You made your decision years ago. I've accepted it and moved on. And, yeah sure, does having you around remind me of a time when things were good? Sure it does. I'd be lying if I said it didn't. But, I have a good man in my life. One who's been there for us because he wanted to be. I trust him and I'm in love with him. To think right now he's home, recovering from a car accident, while I'm over here listening to you play the violin over a box of letters that you wrote because you were feeling a little sad on the road. The truth, Ben, is that's what happens when you have a guilty conscience. You lay on your pillow and cry at night, maybe even take out a pen and record a few thoughts. But when you really love someone, and you're not out for selfish gain, you snap out of it, pack your things, and head home on the fastest thing moving. That's what you do when you're in love."

"But, Mack, I —"

"I know. You tried calling. You did everything short of flying back home and searching high and low until you could find me. Ben, do you know how many nights I dreamt about you showing up and apologizing? I would've accepted you back so fast... back then. But not now. And this whole move with buying the house. I'm not sure if part of it is your way of trying to make up for lost time or what. But, if that's what you're trying to do, please direct all that energy toward Stephanie. She needs and deserves the love and attention of her father. Not me."

Mack could hear the thumping sound of her heartbeat

racing out of control. She didn't know why it took so much courage to be honest with him, but she was proud that she did.

"I see," he said, looking slightly off in another direction.

"I'm sure it's not what you want to hear, but I think it's only fair that I'm honest. Brody is an important part of our lives, and when he's better, I think that you should meet him. Stephanie looks up to him and I think it would be very helpful for her to see all of us getting along."

"Sure. My intentions toward my daughter will never change, Mack. If meeting this guy is important to her and to you, then I'll comply."

"I appreciate it, Ben. We'll be in touch. I'm sure Stephanie will want to set up something again soon. Maybe after your trip?" she asked.

"Sounds good."

CHAPTER 10

"Brody, how are you feeling, love?" Mackenzie asked in a soft voice, gliding her feet across the sheets as she laid with the phone in her hand.

"I've had better days. The pain in my lower back is excruciating, but I'm sure with the help of a heating pad and painkillers, I'll be fine."

"I feel terrible that you're over there by yourself. Brody, I know our last visit didn't exactly end on a high note, but I'm still willing to cook for you. I can make something for the entire week if you'd like. "

"That won't be necessary. Mike and Clara dropped by and brought a few things. They even left the company truck for me to use until I get a new car."

"I see. How nice of them," she replied.

"Yep. Listen, Mack, I thank you for reaching out, but everything is good on this end. Besides, I figured you'd be tied up with Stephanie and your ex at your weekend outing."

Silence ricocheted through the phone to the point of being awkward.

"That's one of the reasons I called to talk with you, Brody. Of course, if you're tired and would rather I call back tomorrow, I'd completely understand." She offered.

"In my present state, all I have is time on my hands. What's on your mind?"

Mackenzie sat upright, looking at herself in the mirror, trying to find the courage for what she was about to say. "I think it's time we had a talk about Ben."

On the other end of the line, she could hear an ever so faint grunt.

"You were right the other day when you said I hadn't set boundaries with Ben. While there's no excuse, I honestly don't think I knew how." She explained.

"I'm not sure I'm following."

"Well, I've never been in a position like this before. It's difficult having your past show up unexpectedly and knowing precisely what to do."

"Mackenzie, are you referring to not knowing how to respond to Ben as Stephanie's father or not knowing how to respond to Ben your ex-husband?"

Again, the line fell silent, making her wish she at least had the television making noise in the background.

"Both."

"Mmm. Somehow, I'm not surprised," he said.

"Brody, I know you've been scorned in your past, but I'm not those other women. Ben and I have a history together. Even though I can't stand what he did, it doesn't mean all the history dissipated into thin air. If I'm being honest with you, I found myself struggling with old emotions and questions that had been harbored for years. I may have buried those old thoughts, but that didn't make them non-existent." She explained.

"What kind of old thoughts? No, wait a minute. Don't answer, allow me to guess. I'll bet you remembered the good times… the way things used to be. Plus, with him being good looking, and a so-called super star, I'm sure it makes it easy to forget all the wrong he's done."

Mack could hear the slight air of disdain in his voice, fully realizing that it wasn't all directed at her. It was directed toward every woman who'd ever let him down. Her mind flashed to the images in her head from the night he told her about his last girlfriend. Brody caught her in the act of cheating. Something a man could never forget. Although her situation didn't come nearly as close, she still understood.

"The honest answer is yes, Brody. I thought about the beginning for a moment. Wondering how things ever went the way they did. It didn't help that Ben tried his best to express that he still has feelings, which I still find to be insane. But, love, I swear. Tonight, I set him straight letting him know that there's only one person for me, and that person is you."

"I don't know, Mack. What makes you so certain? I sat you down and laid my heart on the line, making it clear that I was ready to have the talk with Stephanie, but you resisted. You hadn't been that way prior to Ben showing up. Then in the hospital, I poured my heart out to you again, asking you if everything was okay. You reassured me it was, but I knew deep down that it really wasn't. One of the worst feelings in the world is when you start to realize just how much of a gullible fool you've been. That's how I felt, gullible and angry that guy ever stepped foot on this Island. But then I realized it's not his fault. He can only get away with whatever you will allow. Plus, it would be selfish of me not to consider Stephanie. She really deserves to have her biological father in her life. That's when I decided to step out of the way."

Mackenzie felt the back of her neck, which was moistened with sweat. For the first time since she'd known Brody, she questioned if he'd really consider leaving.

"I realize I could've gone about this differently. But, I'm being honest with you, Brody, laying everything on the line. After the carnival, Ben drove us to a home he'd purchased over the weekend. He even shared a box of letters that he wrote to me and Stephanie over his years of traveling. I haven't read mine and I don't know that I ever will. But what I do know is I stood proud and tall, letting him know that I already had someone special in my life and that I hoped you two could meet once you were feeling better. I also told him he needs to focus all his time and energy toward Stephanie. She's the one who needs him. Not me. I may have stumbled along the way, but I'm on this telephone line with you now, standing firm and sure-footed about the position of my heart. I love you, Brody. You and only you."

She waited quietly with her eyelids closed, flashing back to their first date. It was his smile as he opened the cooler, proud to show her the lunch he'd packed. Then she recalled tidbits of their conversation, and the ultimate dare, causing them both to go semi-skinny dipping in the Patuxent River. It was his humble nature and the fact that he wasn't a ladies' man that did it for Mackenzie.

"Brody, are you still there?"

"I'm here. I appreciate you being straight with me and sharing what's been going on. But I think the best thing to do for now is to allow the dust to settle. Let Ben and Stephanie have their time together and give yourself time to adjust to him living here on the Island. I'm almost certain his presence will be life changing for the two of you, and I wouldn't feel comfortable getting in the way."

"Brody, that isn't necessary. Do you know how broken-hearted Steph would be if you weren't around?"

He cleared his throat. "You know, Mackenzie, I've come to learn a lot about myself over these last couple of months. I've realized that I still have a lot of growing to do if I'm ever going to be in a long-term relationship. I need to grow in the area of trust and vulnerability. Two things that every man and woman should possess in order to strengthen their bond. If Stephanie wants to spend time with me, I'm more than happy to. God knows I love her. But, as for you, I can't help but wonder if you'd miss me just as much as Steph. Or if what we have is finally drawing near to an end."

Everything faded to black as Mackenzie closed her eyes. Whatever remaining words he spoke were muffled in her mind. She tried to imagine what life would be like without Brody in it, then shook herself, not able to accept it. Maybe she hadn't done a good job at communicating with Brody, but she knew one thing for certain. Things couldn't end like this.

CHAPTER 11

Mae watched little children as they played house on the beach and built sandcastles. It had been a while since she took a day to relax. This particular afternoon, she'd responded to Meredith's invite for lunch with the ladies and found herself quite content, hidden under a huge umbrella wearing the largest beach hat she could find.

"Retired life suits you well, Meredith. I only wish I had this kind of free time on my hands throughout the week," she said.

"You say that now, Mae. But wait until it actually happens. It took a long time for me to get used to my newfound freedom. In the beginning, I missed the job and felt lonely."

Edith set down her soda. "That makes two of us. I'm not retired, per se, but I did walk away from the divorce with enough to live comfortably. Of course, money does absolutely nothing to solve loneliness. So, I interviewed and landed a job at Solomons Boutique. I start in a couple of weeks," she said.

"That's sounds like the perfect job for you, Edith. From what I can tell, fashion comes naturally to you," Mae replied.

"Why, thank you."

Mae sank her teeth into another piece of barbecue from Agnes' new food truck. It had become a popular spot among the residents of Solomons, sometimes completely running out of food before the day was complete. "It's the barbecue sauce for me. Whatever ingredients she's using is enough to keep anybody coming back for more. If she keeps cooking like this, she'll need to hire more people to help keep up with the demand."

"You got that right. The ribs are absolutely delicious." Meredith agreed.

Mae nodded. "You know, ladies. I have to thank you for coming together like this. I probably should be embarrassed to admit it, but I don't really have any friends. At least not outside of Jonathan, who's my husband and best friend, but even we're at odds as of late." She confessed.

"You and Jonathan are having trouble in paradise? I can't imagine the two of you not getting along. Not with the way you're always so lovey dovey with each other." Meredith smiled.

Mae chuckled. "Oh, trust me, we'll get back to normal once we get past this little rough patch. But it's times like these that make me realize how I need to get away and recharge. As it stands, I'm either at work or at home with Jonathan. While I love my husband and my job, sometimes I just need a break. Even if it's just for an hour."

"Amen, sister! My famous saying is balance in all things. When I was married, I took care of everything but myself. Not a wise move on my part. Needless to say, after years of neglecting self-care, here I am trying to make up for lost time." Edith confessed.

"Do you think you'd ever get married again?" Mae asked.

"Maybe if the right man came along, sure. I'd like to think I've learned a few lessons that might serve me well in a future relationship. If one could only be so lucky, like Meredith, to actually meet a nice man," Edith said, winking over at Meredith.

Mae fanned a paper napkin toward Meredith. "You haven't mentioned a word about Theodore as of late. How are things going with you two? We want to hear every detail. I know I've seen his car parked in your driveway at least twice in the past week." Mae teased.

Meredith crossed her legs, fanning herself with a huge smile on her face. "We may have enjoyed an outing or two this week. However, I'm a lady, therefore I don't kiss and tell."

"Oh, so you kissed him?" Mae asked.

Meredith playfully rolled her eyes. "Fine, if you're going to sit here and twist my arm, I might as well share. Theodore has been such a gentleman. He took me to the new restaurant by the water the other night. We had a candlelight dinner and a view that was to die for. He treated me like a queen, something I haven't experienced in a long time."

"Isn't that wonderful? See there. A woman never knows when she's going to meet her guy. It may be someone you've crossed paths with a thousand times and had absolutely no idea," Mae said.

Meredith folded her eyebrows like an accordion. "Yes, but there's only one thing about Theodore that strikes me as odd."

"What is it?"

"He hasn't tried to kiss me yet. Not one single attempt. We went on the boat ride with you and Jonathan, we've been out to eat. I've even had him over to the house a time or two. You'd think by now he'd go for a little peck on the lips. Maybe even a kiss on the cheek if he was feeling kind of shy."

Edith choked on her beverage for a quick moment before pulling it together. "No kissing? That's interesting. Does he at least flirt with you?" she asked.

Mae raised her hand. "I can answer that one. I witnessed the two of them together and from what I saw, kissing should not be an issue."

Meredith drew herself toward the edge of her chair. "Well, it is," she whispered while looking around. "At first, I thought it was me. You know, maybe my breath was off-putting, but I checked. I carry more mints in my purse than the law should allow." Meredith explained.

"Yes, but do you put them in your mouth?" Edith asked, causing everyone but Meredith to burst into laughter.

"Oh, Edith, hush. Of course, I do."

Mae held her stomach, trying her best to control her laughter. Quietly, she noticed how nice it was getting to know Meredith from this perspective. A point of view she hadn't experienced before now. "Now, now, ladies. All jokes aside. Maybe he's just taking his time with you out of respect. I'm sure he wants to show you how much of a gentleman he can be. The one thing we know for certain is he's interested. If he wasn't into you, then he wouldn't repeatedly take you out," Mae said.

"That's a good point. I suppose I'll need to be patient. However, I don't know how much longer I can hold out. The way he holds my hand, makes me laugh, and the way he smells when he gives me a hug," she said, nearly quivering in her chair.

"Somebody is smitten." Edith teased.

"I'm just having a good time, that's all. Is there anything wrong with two adults enjoying one another's company?" Meredith asked.

"If that's what you'd like to believe, then you go with that. In my world, we call it being smitten," Mae said, agreeing with Edith.

"Yeah, well, enough about me. I'm curious to know what's

going on with you and Jonathan. Is everything okay between you two?" Meredith asked.

"For the most part. We just can't seem to settle on where we want to retire. We have five more years, but that time will go by in the blink of an eye, and when it does, I want to stay right here on the Island. Jonathan seems to think we'd be better off in a place like Florida. In my opinion, it's a terrible idea." She explained.

Meredith waved her off like it was a foolish debate. "Why? I'd live in the sunshine state in a heartbeat. It's far less expensive, that's for sure."

Mae packed up her bag of leftovers and stretched out on her lounge chair, dangling one leg so she could dig her feet in the sand. "Now, you sound like Jonathan. Money isn't everything, you know. Especially when it comes to family. I'd like to be as close to them as possible. I have my daughter Lily and the grandkids to think about. As it is, we don't see each other often, and moving further away would only make it worse."

Mae drifted, recalling the way life was when her late husband was living and they were raising Lily. They sent her to the best of schools, made sure she was active in the community, and provided her with the best life had to offer. Now that Lily was a mother, Mae couldn't blame her for trying to do the same for the grandkids in New Jersey.

Edith lathered herself in more sunscreen while offering advice. "Just make sure you keep the lines of communication open with Jonathan. Maybe he'll come around and see things from your point of view. Whatever you do, talk to each other and listen even more than you talk. That way you can avoid going down the slippery slope that I did at all costs."

"Thank you, Edith, but for now, I'm putting the conversation to rest unless Jonathan brings it up. After all, we do have a few more years before a final decision has to be made. And, right now, I'd love more than anything to just enjoy our fifteen-year celebration. Speaking of which, my boss, Mike, is organizing a little gathering to celebrate fifteen years at Lighthouse Tours. When I find out the details, I'll share, but you two should come."

Meredith laid down her beverage. "Has it been fifteen years already? It seems like just yesterday when you were settling in the house. My goodness."

"Yes, it has. Fifteen years and if I were younger, I would give tours for another fifteen. I can honestly say this has been the most fun job I've ever had. Listening to the passengers talk as they enjoy the tours and sailing to and from the various lighthouse locations never gets old to me." Mae explained.

Again, Mae drifted, recalling the first time she pulled up to Lighthouse Tours, excited about starting a new chapter. All the warm nostalgic memories caused water to well up in her eyes. She didn't know how, but she hoped to convince Jonathan that his idea of leaving would be a terrible mistake.

∽

Mackenzie dropped the last shark's tooth in a bag, winding down her hunting expedition with Stephanie. She begged and pleaded for weeks to visit the cliffs located off Chesapeake Bay. To a young child, collecting fossils sounded adventurous and was growing in popularity among her friends. But, with the afternoon winding down, they'd soon head home and prepare for a relaxing evening.

As Mack drove, thoughts lingered of how she would introduce Ben's letters to Stephanie. This afternoon she'd finally worked up enough courage to mention it, but tonight she'd finally worked up enough courage to give it a try. "Baby, how would you like an oven baked pizza tonight? I was thinking you could help me cover it in your favorite pepperoni topping."

Stephanie smiled. "Can I have double cheese and pepperoni?" she asked.

"Double cheese and pepperoni sounds like a winner to me."

"Cool. Maybe we can even find a movie to watch? I can pop the popcorn." Steph begged in the sweetest voice she could muster up.

"Well, we might have to save movie night for the weekend, love. Mom has to get back to work early in the morning. I had tons of fun with you at the cliffs, but I can't take off two days in a row. Joshua would have a cow." Mack explained.

Steph giggled, likely taking the figure of speech literally. "When are we going to see Brody? It feels like he's been sick for a long time. Maybe he needs a slice of pizza to help him feel better."

"It hasn't been that long, Stephanie. It takes the body a while to heal. Plus —" She hesitated. "Now that your dad is moving to Solomons Island, Brody was thinking you might want to spend some extra time with him."

Mack glanced in the rearview at her daughter, who was wearing sunglasses and looking all grown up.

"I can spend time with Dad and Brody. We should introduce them to one another. Daddy is real nice and Brody is real nice, so they would probably be good friends."

"I understand, Steph, but it isn't always as easy for adults the way it is with children," Mack replied.

She watched as Stephanie removed her glasses. "What do you mean?"

Mackenzie released a long sigh, wishing there wasn't more to explain, and uncertain how her eight-year-old would take it in the first place. "Nothing, love. I'm probably overthinking everything. What I do know is your dad asked me to pass along a very special gift to you. It's something he's been saving for you since you were a little baby."

"What is it?"

Mackenzie gripped the wheel, searching for the right words. "It's a treasure chest filled with letters that he wrote to you while he was traveling on the road." She explained.

"A chest full of treasures?"

"Um, not quite, love. More like a shoebox filled with letters. But the letters are a treasure from your dad's heart." Mack smiled.

"Oh, can I read them tonight?"

"Sure, but there are a lot of letters. He arranged them by date, so how about you read one or two before bed? Maybe it's something you can do each night during your last few weeks of summer vacation." She suggested.

"Okay."

Mack glanced in the mirror again, watching a serious expression wash over Stephanie's face.

"Mom?"

"Yes, love."

"Were you ever mad at Daddy for leaving to travel with his band?"

Mackenzie clamped her teeth together looking straight ahead at the road. "I wanted to support your dad as he fulfilled his dreams, love. But I would've been most happy if your dad would've found a way to work on his dreams while staying with the family so he could watch you grow up. It's just not the way things turned out." She explained.

"Are you still mad at Daddy now?"

In that moment Mackenzie realized her little girl understood more than she thought. She was growing up. A child beyond her years, who was as gentle as a lamb and as discerning as an adult who'd walked the earth for years.

"Not anymore, sweetheart. I'm happy your father was able to fulfill his dreams, and I'm most happy he's able to spend more time getting to know you."

"Hmm." Steph grunted.

"Oh, boy. What else is on that sweet little mind of yours?"

"Would you ever marry Daddy again?"

Mack glanced in the rear-view mirror for a second time, watching her daughter's sweet little face as she stared out the window.

"No, honey. There are only two people that hold a special place in my heart. You first —"

"And Brody?" she asked, sounding upbeat.

"Yes, love. How would you feel if Brody ever asked me to marry him someday? Do you think you would like the idea of him being your stepdad?"

"You mean I could have two dads? That would make me the luckiest girl in all of Solomons Elementary!"

Mackenzie hooked a left turn into the street where they lived, smiling big at the idea that having two dads gave Stephanie such joy.

∽

After putting Stephanie to bed, Mackenzie flopped on the couch, noticing the second shoebox labeled with her name. She had half a mind to get rid of it, knowing that nothing that Ben wrote could persuade her or change her feelings.

She looked up, noticing it was just after the eleven o'clock hour.

No missed calls or messages from Brody. Man, he must really be upset, she thought, combing her fingers through her hair. Sending a quick text was always an option, but she wanted more than that. She needed to see him.

Mackenzie leaned forward, opening the lid to her box, noticing the first letter on top was dated seven years prior. If her letters were anything like Stephanie's had been, she was in for a lot of talk about what life was like on the road.

'Dear Mack, Where do I begin? Words cannot express how sorry I am. To think almost an entire year has gone by is absolutely heart wrenching to me. I tried every way I know how to call and find you. I figured if I could send you what little bit of money I had to help out, it would be something to carry you until the band starts bringing in more income. I left messages with your family as well. So far no one seems to be willing to reveal where you've moved, which is understandable since they're all probably pretty upset with me. There's no excuse for what I've done. If you were standing before me right now asking why I left, there's only one answer I could possibly give. I simply believed I would never be good at anything else unless I was able to fulfill my God-given talent. It sounds selfish, I know, but I believed I would never be the kind of provider that you and Stephanie deserved while wearing a suit and tie. I felt confined working nine to five at a dead-end job, with no room for growth. It wasn't for me. I wasn't skilled and talented enough to climb the corporate ladder. The only talent I truly possessed was with my vocals and my instruments. Sadly, the consequences to my decision have been great. As I sit here on the back of an old bus with my guitar and my dreams of making it big, I feel like I have a world of options ahead of me, but none of it means anything without my family. I know you may never believe me, but I'll take my chances and share with you anyway. I promise from the core of my very being, that as soon as I make it, I'm coming back for you and my girl. I'm coming back to give you both the life that you deserve...'

Mackenzie continued reading several more pages with dry eyes and very little emotion. All she could recall were flashbacks to what life was like raising a child alone.

She placed the letter back in the box and closed the lid. As far as she was concerned, there was no reason to continue reading further.

CHAPTER 12

"I'm done with relationships. Seems like I'd do a much better job at just flying solo." Brody tossed a tool onto the counter and walked around, searching for his toolbox.

"Have you lost your mind? Wait. Before you answer that, let's start with why you're here in the first place. The North Beach office and the Solomons Island office are supposed to be off limits to you until your back heals," Mike responded.

Every ache and pain in Brody's body mostly resided within his lower back, giving him daily reminders of the accident. He'd given up on painkillers, knowing they could be addictive, but the idea of therapy was starting to cross his mind every now and again.

"Mike, I know you're looking out for me, but if I spend day in and day out staring at my ceiling, I'm going to drive myself insane. So far, all the heating pads and painkillers in the world haven't done a thing for me. If I'm going to be miserable, I might as well be while working here at the North Beach office."

He observed Mike watching him out of his peripheral vision but refused to make eye contact.

"Okay, Mr. Stubborn. Have it your way, but I better not see you lifting anything heavier than that wrench you have in your hand. On second thought, just stick to paperwork for this week. Working on repairs requires all kinds of unnecessary bending and lifting. That I will not allow until your doctor gives the okay," he said.

"I think you can trust my judgement, Mike. I won't overdo it."

Mike slid over a stool, placing it behind Brody. "Take a load off. Trusting your judgment is something I normally would do, but I think the remnants of those pain killers are still having an effect. Now, what's this I hear you saying about being done with women? Again, I ask, are you nuts? You're dating the best of the best. What's the problem now?"

Brody knew Mackenzie was the best. She wasn't the problem. It was her sly ex-husband showing up, trying to stake a claim on his woman after all these years. That was the problem in his eyes.

"History." Brody grumbled.

"What?"

"They have history. I can't compete with that. It doesn't matter how good your woman is. When someone from your past shows up, specifically someone who you share a child with, that knocks the other guy right out of the running. Again, it's what they call history, and because of their history, I don't stand a chance." He groaned, tossing his tool down, then picking up a clipboard in its place.

"Is that what Mackenzie told you?"

With his back still facing Mike, Brody wrote on the top of the form and began going over an itemized list. "Is Jan still sitting at the front desk? She only gave me the inventory sheet for the month of July. I need the sheets from June as well," he said, trying his best to deflect from the question.

"Brody, did she say that or are you just making things up in your head?"

"She may as well have said it. I already told you she hasn't been herself ever since he came into town. I asked her again and again if anything was wrong and all I got was silence up until this week. She keeps talking about being confused or not knowing how to handle this or that. If it was me, I'd stand up to the guy and say hey, look buddy, you can have a relationship with your daughter, but that's it, I'm taken."

Brody tried to fight back the heat rising in his neck just talking about it. He put the chart down and continued. "Look, at this point what's done is done. Her lack of clarity is all I need to know it's time to move on. Besides, some guys are naturals when it comes to relationships. Me, not so much. I was probably a fool for getting involved to begin with."

He felt Mike pacing around the room and wished he'd never broached the topic.

"I understand your feelings are hurt, Brody, but there are some things in life that are worth fighting for. Don't you think Mackenzie falls into that category?"

"I value everything about Mackenzie. But how I feel doesn't mean a darn thing if she no longer feels the same way about me."

"Come on, man. You don't really think she stopped loving you overnight, do you? I'd like to think you two mean so much more to each other," Mike replied.

Brody swallowed, feeling a lump welling up in his throat the size of a miniature golf ball.

"Feelings can change, Mike. Not only do I lack the history, but I can't offer her and Stephanie the life that he can. I looked the guy up. He seems pretty popular among the ladies, and I'm sure he has a bankroll to back up his popularity."

Mike pulled up another stool next to Brody's and crossed his arms, staring at the wall in front of them.

"You can have all the money in the world, but it can't buy genuine love, my friend. Give her a little time. If I know her right, Mackenzie will come around. For as long as we've been doing business in Solomons, she's been nothing but a solid individual, respected by many. Clara would back me on that any day of the week. She's the real deal, Brody."

"Mmm hmm."

Mike continued. "Now, instead of us sitting here staring at this wall, do you mind telling me something?" he asked.

"What's that?"

"Of all the office locations, how did you end up choosing to come to North Beach, instead of Solomons? I'm sure Jan appreciates the additional company, but didn't I have you scheduled at Solomons for the month of July?"

"Yeah, about that. I was hoping you'd cut me some slack for the next couple of weeks. I promise to see to it that everything gets done in a timely fashion, but I just needed a little time away from Solomons." He explained.

"Time away from what?"

Brody rose off the stool and paced to the other side of the work counter to keep from getting too stiff.

"Oh, I get it. You didn't want to risk the chance of running into Mack. Is that it?" Mike probed.

"Something like it. I just need a little peace and quiet for a while. The fewer reminders of our current situation the better," he replied, pausing in front of the window that faced a nearby pier.

"Hmm, interesting. Brody, I'm assuming you know what you're doing. At the end of the day, you're the one in the relationship and not me. Therefore, I won't interfere any further. Take as much time as you need to sort things out. But I do want to offer you one word of caution."

"Mike, do you have to? I don't mean any harm, but I came here to help clear my mind. Not make it worse," Brody said, sounding melancholy.

"I understand that, but please hear me out. If you're really in love with her, you need to fight with everything you have. This is no time to give into whatever your pride and your ego are telling you to do. Now, that's it, my friend. I love you like a brother, therefore everything I'm saying is coming from a good place."

Brody sighed. He believed Mike, but it was going to take an act of congress to build up his confidence and expose his heart again.

Mike got up and pushed his stool in. "On another note, there's one more thing we need to tackle by the end of the week. Jonathan and Mae are celebrating fifteen years of service with the company. We've invited the entire Solomons' office and North Beach's to attend a cocktail hour with heavy hors d'oeuvre. The celebration will be this Friday on the rooftop of the Charles Street Restaurant on the Island. Do you think you'll be able to make it?" he asked.

"Sure, I don't see why not. I may spend the majority of the time in a chair, but I wouldn't miss celebrating those two for anything in the world," Brody responded.

"Good, we look forward to having you. Oh, and one more thing —"

"Gee, Mike, you're just full of surprises today, aren't you?"

"I guess. However, this one is to be expected. Mackenzie and the crew from the café will be there as well. You might want to think on what we talked about by then. Or not. It's up to you." Mike exited the room, leaving the weight of the entire conversation on his shoulders for him to contemplate.

∽

Later that afternoon, Mae spread a towel out, making a space for herself to eat next to Jonathan. He sat with his legs dangling off the dock, testing out a new set of fishing rods. Something he did on occasion in preparation for his afternoon tours.

"Do you mind if I join you?" she asked.

"Be my guest. I won't be here much longer, anyway."

She popped open her soda can and took a swig before responding. "Jonathan, I think it's about time we break our silence, don't you?" she said, watching as he continued fiddling with his fishing rod as if he didn't have any other cares in the world.

"I'm not giving you the silent treatment, Mae. I simply don't have anything to say that would be of value to you, that's all," he replied.

"Seriously? Everything you say is of value to me. Now, whether or not I agree with you is a different story." She snorted, hoping he'd find a little humor in it, but he didn't.

"Come on, Jonathan, there has to be a way for the two of us to compromise on the matter. Since when have we ever had a disagreement that we couldn't work out?"

Jonathan stopped what he was doing and finally made eye contact. "You see, that's it. That's the problem in a nutshell. I don't think you understand what compromise really is, Mae. You're only willing to see things from one point of view. If we're being honest, just about every disagreement ends with me coming over to your side, giving in to your way. That's not what I had in mind when we said I do."

Mae slowly removed her soda from her mouth, feeling a

sudden loss of appetite. She assumed she'd sit beside him and break the ice, but she had no idea he felt as strongly as he did.

"Wow, Jonathan, I don't quite know what to say."

"It's fine. I probably said a lot more than I should've in the first place." He grumbled.

No matter how many times Mae considered moving to Florida since their last conversation, her heart was attached to the Island. She figured she'd give Jonathan a little time to get used to the idea of staying, and like always, he'd just come around.

"So, you're really serious about wanting to leave, aren't you?" she asked.

"Yes, Mae. I am. Why else would I go as far as telling you if I didn't really mean it? I've always been honest with you. Even prior to getting married, when we were just friends. I've always been the one with an adventurous spirit. You knew that about me then, and you know this about me now. I'm not saying we can't spend time with the family. That's exactly why we bought the boat last year, so we could spend more time with the ones we love and travel with them. But, to disregard my feelings, just because you're comfortable living here on the Island forever... well, in my opinion, that's simply not fair."

Mae would not give into her emotions. Instead, she wrapped her lunch in the paper bag and spoke in an even-keeled tone. "So, that's what this is about, Jonathan, adventure? I thought I was rather supportive when you wanted to be adventurous and purchase the boat. If it were up to me, the funds would've remained tucked away for safekeeping."

"You came around to loving the idea, Mae." He offered.

"Yes, after I realized I had no choice because you'd already made the purchase. All that is hindsight now, but it leaves me wondering what this is really all about. The same way I knew when we got married you were adventurous, was the same way you knew I was a homebody, happy tending to my garden and operating within the familiar. Now, you want to take me away from everything I know? All in the name of adventure?"

Jonathan wore a long face as he put his equipment down, seemingly no longer interested in testing it out.

"Anna Mae Middleton, all I want to know is that you have my back just as much as I have yours. That's what this is all about. I would go to the moon and back for you. But would you do the same for me? My desire to move south is about more than adventure. We can save money if we move and live a good life."

"That's all well and good, Jonathan, but we already have a good life right here in Solomons." She argued.

"Yes, we do, and it works for now because we're still working. When we're retired, I'd like to think you don't want to give all of our funds away to property taxes and a high cost of living. I love living on the Island just as much as you do, but we can find another place by the water that will meet your needs just fine. But, in order to do that, you have to be willing and open-minded." He explained.

For the first time, the unthinkable crossed her mind. She wondered if their differences on such an important topic would be the cause for going their separate ways.

No, Mae, get that out of your mind.

"I guess there's a lot to be said about growing old and getting settled in your ways. I'll be the first to admit it. I'm too old to move, and it will take an act of God to get me to consider otherwise. I like traveling the same route to the same grocery store and back. I enjoy my weekend routines, my gardening, and the same old stubborn soil of Solomons Island that continuously grows wild weeds in my backyard every summer. I'll also be the first to admit that I do not want to move. I never have and I never will."

In her mind, she imagined the banging sound of a gavel, feeling internally fired up about the subject. She also knew the moment the words slipped out, she had already said too much, digging herself in a hole she would have a hard time getting out of.

"I see," he replied.

"That's it? Don't you have more to say?"

"No. Not a word. It's like I said in the beginning. There's nothing I have to offer that would be of value to you."

"Come on, Jonathan. That's not true and you know it. We're just hashing out our differences. In the end, we'll come up with something that's workable for the two of us."

She watched as Jonathan got up and gathered his belongings. "Jonathan?"

"I think I better head inside and grab a quick bite before it's time for me to start the next tour."

"Jonathan, you can't just walk away. We're in the middle of an important conversation," she said.

He cleared his throat. "You stated your point and made yourself pretty clear. You're not leaving. Therefore, there's nothing more for me to say."

"Well, what about our party on Friday? We can't go and freely enjoy ourselves if we leave this conversation lingering over our heads."

Jonathan took several steps away before stopping with his back facing in her direction.

"It will be fine, Mae. We can put the conversation to rest and pretend like it never happened. I'm going to head inside. I'll see you at home."

The back door to Lighthouse Tours slammed shut after Jonathan made a subtle yet grand exit, leaving Mae with unresolved feelings.

~

Mackenzie held back her pride, making her way through the crowd over to Brody. Her thought process was to do and say anything she could to get back in his good graces… better yet, to get him back for good.

He sat alone at a table, likely to stay out of the way of those enjoying themselves at Mae and Jonathan's party. And probably to avoid additional back pain. "Hey, stranger."

He looked handsome from her point of view, wearing his best plaid button-down shirt with a tie. "Hi, Mackenzie. I didn't realize you were here," he said.

It was a simple one liner, but all she could think about was how much of a fool she'd been in recent weeks. Not that it was ever intentional. She loved Brody. But she still could've done a better job at not allowing Ben to come along and trigger old emotions.

"How could I miss it? Fifteen years of loyal service to one company is such an honorable accomplishment. When Mike called to invite me to their little soiree, I didn't hesitate to say yes. I sure hope to be like Mae and Jonathan when I grow up. Look at them. They're best friends, successful, and in love. It doesn't get any better than that." She smiled, looking over at Mae and Jonathan as they greeted their guests.

"Interesting," he replied.

"What?"

"I should've known Mike would invite some of the people from the community. When that guy says he throwing a small gathering, you can assume he means the opposite." Brody explained, laughing til his back made him flinch.

She didn't know whether to take that as a sign that he was happy to see her or not. "Oh, Brody. Are you sure you shouldn't pay your doctor a visit? You look like you're in the same amount of pain as you were in the night of the accident. That's no way to live."

He waved it off. "I'll be fine. I placed a few calls and will be going to see a specialist at the beginning of next week. Enough about me. How's Stephanie doing? Is she with her sitter tonight? Or maybe her father?" he asked, with the last word dwindling down to barely a whisper.

"She's with the sitter. And, for the record, she misses you so much, Brody. Every time I turn around, she's asking when she'll have a chance to spend some time with you."

A lazy smile emerged across Brody's face, making Mack at least feel comfortable enough to pull up a chair and sit down.

"Do you think it would be okay if I brought her by sometime?"

"Sure. I wouldn't mind seeing Stephanie. I'd hoped she wouldn't forget about me," he replied, looking out among the crowd.

"Forget about you? Are you kidding me? You played such an integral role in her life. You play, I should say. There's no way in the world Steph could ever forget you."

She took note as Brody tapped his finger on the table, either nervously or somewhat agitated, she wasn't sure. All Mackenzie knew was there was work to be done if she was going to make any headway with him tonight.

He looked her straight in the eye and said, "You probably said it right the first time... I may have played a role in her life, but I understand the importance of stepping aside and making room for the most important man in her life. Stephanie needs her father."

"I can't argue with you on that, but she also needs you. Whether you like it or not, you already won my little girl's heart. She loves you, Brody, with every ounce of her being. I also love you, so if you think you can easily get rid of us, you'll have to think again."

Brody let out a deep sigh. "Please don't do this, Mackenzie. You must think I'm blind not to see that your ex won your heart as well. The writing on the wall was beyond plain to see."

"What are you talking about, Brody? I don't think you're blind at all. I've been very transparent with you about everything that I was going through."

He cut her a look that she hadn't seen before. "Everything?"

"Well, okay. I could've done a better job at telling you right away when Ben asked me about buying a house on the Island. And I should've introduced you to him by now, I get it. But I needed time to take it all in, to figure out what it all meant, and how I would proceed going forward." She scrambled, feeling as if her plan to profess her love was beginning to tumble down a slippery slope.

Brody stood upright. "It's okay, you really don't have to explain. Sometimes things take a turn in an unexpected direction."

Mackenzie could feel a burning sensation rising in her eyes. Refusing to give into defeat, she walked around the table to Brody and tasted his soft lips, silencing him from any additional negativity.

She continuously drew in his lower and upper lip, and he responded with passion, just as he always had.

The sound of a man clearing his throat reverberated, interrupting their physical connection. "Well, well, well. What do we have here?" Mike asked, with Clara standing beside him.

"Sorry, boss," Brody responded, straightening himself up.

Mack made eye contact with him as he apologized but didn't say a word.

"No need to apologize. We were hoping the two of you

would run into each other, isn't that right, Clara?" He chuckled.

"Yep. I hear there's an observation deck one floor below. Maybe after Jonathan and Mae give their speech, you two should get lost for a little while. Go and take a walk. I'm sure they'd understand," she said.

Mackenzie could see the hesitation written across Brody's face. "It's fine. We don't have to go anywhere," she said, figuring she'd give him an out. Besides, after all the effort she was making to express her love, if it wasn't good enough for him anymore, then perhaps she should call it quits.

"It's not that I don't want to. I just can't with my back. I have to calculate my steps carefully, if you know what I mean." He smiled.

Relief washed over her like a cool shower on a hot summer night. "Of course, your back! We can always take a raincheck on the observation deck, Brody. I'm just happy to be here with you." Mackenzie explained.

"I'm happy you're here as well. I could be wrong, but somehow, I think Mike orchestrated all this," he said, glancing over at Mike. "Either way, I'm thankful, but I still think we need to talk... alone."

"Sure," Mack replied, except this time he was the one who slipped her a kiss. A refreshing feeling after all the tension and confusion.

CHAPTER 13

Mae lifted the microphone standing on the podium and motioned for Jonathan to join her. "Good evening, everyone. As Jonathan makes his way to the front, I just wanted to publicly thank Mike." She smiled, welcoming Jonathan by her side.

The chatter in the background simmered down. "As much as Mike would like to make a fuss over our fifteen years of service, we would be remiss if we didn't thank him for providing us with such a pleasant working experience. It's not often you get to work at a place with such a family-oriented environment. It's the recipe that makes Lighthouse Tours so special, and the reason why we're still here today." She explained, passing the mic to Jonathan.

As he began speaking, Mae surveyed the crowd, noticing the staff from the North Beach office, a few of the local business owners, and of course, their very own Mike and Clara.

"I'd have to agree wholeheartedly with my wife. But, if we're going to tell it right, this journey began long before we came to the Island. I'm sure many of you know this, but Mike hired us way back during our days of working in Annapolis. That's where the true magic began. It's the same place where Mae and I began as co-workers, then became friends, and eventually we landed here and became husband and wife. You don't hear too many stories like that nowadays."

Whistling sounds exploded from the back of the room.

"Ha, thank you. Perhaps there's something to be said about Lighthouse Tours being the place for lovers. It's also the same establishment where Mike and Clara formed their union." Jonathan chuckled.

The crowd cheered, making the young couple blush.

"Mike, a sincere thank you to you and the employees of Lighthouse Tours for making our time here so memorable," Jonathan said.

Mike raised his hands to his mouth, yelling out, "Hold on a minute, this is starting to sound like a goodbye speech. We still have at least five more years to go... maybe even more," he said, making the crowd break out into harmonious laughter.

Mae took over the mic. "Is that a guaranteed offer? If so, sign us up. Jonathan and I would be happy to stay planted here in Solomons." She smiled toward Jonathan and immediately noticed a shift in his demeanor. One that he was trying to stifle, but she knew her husband. "All right, everyone, a little birdie told me there's a delicious cake to enjoy. Please help yourselves, and again, thank you for coming out to celebrate this joyous occasion with us!"

Mae reattached the mic and followed Jonathan, giving everyone they met along the way a warm greeting. She realized in the midst of shaking hands and greeting people, he was really exiting the floor. "Jonathan, where are you going? We haven't had cake yet," she said, calling after him.

"I'm going to grab some air. I'll be back."

"Jonathan... Jonathan —" She repeated, while discretely trying to follow him.

The elevator door opened, and she followed him in, feeling embarrassed that some could see them leaving. Once the doors closed, she let him have it.

"What on earth, Jonathan? We're the guests of honor. How could you just walk out like that?" she asked.

"Mae, I said I needed to get some fresh air. I plan on coming back."

"Last time I checked, we were already outside. I'd hate for Mike and Clara to think we're not grateful. How many employees do you hear of that receive such a celebration prior to retirement? Especially after all the money they had to spend correcting the error I made on their account. For goodness' sake, you can't be serious, Jonathan."

The door opened to the main lobby where customers waited to be seated in the regular restaurant. The panoramic views of the Chesapeake Bay were to die for.

Mae followed Jonathan to the parking lot. "Okay, now that we're out here, do you mind telling me what's gotten into you?"

Jonathan slid his hands in his pockets, maintaining his composure as he quoted her line by line. "'Jonathan and I would be happy to stay planted here in Solomons'. Do you think I can't read between the lines, Mae? That sounded like a direct message, letting all of us know how serious you are about remaining in the area. After the discussions we've been having as of late, one would think you'd approach the topic with a lot more sensitivity." He grumbled.

Mae closed her eyes to keep from rolling them. "That's what sent you storming out of the party? Jonathan, our co-workers, friends, and neighbors are all here to celebrate with us. I can't believe you left over that."

"I didn't storm out, Mae. I spoke to everyone along the way and told you I needed fresh air. You made the choice to follow."

Mae shifted nervously, knowing the best approach was to respond gingerly with honey. But her flesh wanted to tell him this wasn't the time or place.

"Jonathan, I didn't mean it the way you think. It was a lighthearted joke. Mike is looking to train fresh blood, starting in a matter of weeks. I'd never expect in a million years that he'd look to keep us indefinitely."

Jonathan turned away. "I don't know, Mae. Sounds like something you'd suggest, knowing on the back end you'd accomplish your goal of staying here much longer than I planned."

"Sweetheart, that's not what I'm doing at all. If that's the message I wanted to convey, I wouldn't be sneaky or underhanded about it. I'd just come right out and say that I'm not leaving. I haven't done that, have I?" She slipped her hand over the back of his shoulder blade. "I want nothing more than to see you happy... I want us both to be happy. And, for me, happiness entails being with you. Period."

He slowly turned around giving her his undivided attention. "Really?"

"Well, of course. What kind of woman do you think I am?" she asked, smiling real big. "I didn't marry you with the intention of only having my way. Although, in this circumstance I really would like to have my way. I'm sure we can devise a plan that entails visiting the family from Florida or having them fly out to us. The world won't come to an end. Besides, as long as we're together, that's all that matters."

Jonathan appeared to stand frozen for what seemed like a full minute before the words registered in his mind. Even then, he looked at her cautiously, then let out a huge chuckle. "So, you really wouldn't mind moving?"

She slapped his arm with a napkin she'd been holding. "Don't make me say it twice, you old goat." She teased. "I love you, Jonathan, and if loving you means I have to follow you to the end of the earth, I will."

Jonathan slid his hands around her waistline. "Mae, that's all I ever really wanted to hear. For a moment there I thought you were choosing Solomons over me. It may sound a little crazy, but —" He hesitated.

Mae gazed into his eyes. "But what?"

"My whole heart is devoted to you. We may not always agree on everything, but you have every inch of my heart, and I guess I just needed to know that you feel the same way in return." He confessed.

Mae cupped Jonathan's face in between the palm of her hands, "Jonathan Middleton, I want you to listen very carefully to what I'm about to say. Sometimes I'm set in my ways and stubborn. I'll be the first to admit it. But when I committed my life to you, I meant it wholeheartedly. Till death do us part, remember?"

Jonathan smiled. "Of course, I do. It wasn't that long ago."

"Exactly. Now, I teased you earlier, calling you an old goat, but let the truth be told, out of the two of us, I'm the real old goat," she said, bursting into laughter. "You knew this about me, didn't you?"

"Sweetheart, a man would never call his wife an old goat, but yes, I knew you were accustomed to your way of doing things."

Mae planted a kiss on his nose. "Good. Then you'll understand that it takes time for me to get used to new ideas, but that doesn't mean that I love you any less."

Jonathan planted a kiss on her forehead, then her lips. "Thank you, Mae. Sometimes a man just needs to hear the words, that's all. As long as we're together, we can figure out the rest. I love you, darlin."

"I love you too, Jonathan."

~

Toward the end of the party, Mackenzie walked alongside Brody to the pickup he'd borrowed from Mike. She'd patiently waited for a quiet moment where they could speak openly, but she found herself not knowing where to begin.

"I guess you'll be in the market for a new truck soon, maybe something that's a bit of an upgrade from the last one?"

Brody shrugged his shoulders. "Oh, I don't know. I was pretty fond of my old pickup. Somehow the pleather seats and the good old tape deck suited me just fine, mostly because it was payment free. These trucks nowadays cost a nice penny. Not sure if that's the route I want to take this time around."

Half of her still didn't believe he'd been in such a terrible wreck. If it wasn't for his back and the slower pace in which he moved, one might not believe it. In a lot of ways, he was pretty darn lucky, or better yet, blessed according to the way her late grandmother would've phrased it.

He continued. "I'll figure something out. More importantly, I think now's the perfect time to hear what's on your heart and mind. I'd be a fool to continue to pretend like I don't miss you, Mack. But I'd be even more of a fool if I didn't express my concern about you and your ex." He leaned against the crew cab, waiting to hear her response.

"I know, Brody. I now realize what I must've put you through when I hesitated and asked you to put off the conversation with Stephanie. But I can reassure you with absolute conviction that my heart is completely dedicated to you... to us. To prove it, I want you to meet Ben. Unfortunately, he's not going anywhere anytime soon, at least that's what he says. However, Stephanie and I both want you to get to know him. It's important to us, especially if you're going to be her stepdad."

An immediate smile emerged on Brody's face. One she hadn't seen in a long time.

"Wait a minute. Does Steph know this? If so, how does she feel about it? I sure would've appreciated being a part of such an important conversation," he said.

She observed the rigidness washing away from his expression as he returned to the old Brody that she knew and loved. A welcomed and familiar feeling that she wanted to last.

"No, Steph's not aware yet. But I was thinking we could sit down and have the conversation with her. I'm ready, Brody. I'm all in, ready to fulfill our dreams together. You already know how I felt about you prior to Ben's arrival. I hate that things had to go the way they did, but a part of me is grateful for the journey." She explained.

"How so?"

Mackenzie leaned back against the truck beside him. "Well, for starters, I sat with Stephanie, allowing her to read some of the letters Ben wrote to her when he was on the road. I think I briefly mentioned the letters to you a little while back."

"You did."

"Yeah, well, of course, Steph was one hundred percent excited that her dad did something that special for her. But I felt like I could see right through it. He may win over the heart of a little girl, but as for me, not so much. The entire time she read his words out loud, all I could think about was 'where were you when we needed you most.'" She explained.

"I'm sorry. I hate that you had to go through that, but at the end of the day, you're doing what's best for Stephanie. That's all that matters."

Mackenzie rested her head backward, looking up at the stars in the sky. "Yes, but it gets worse. The letters he wrote me... I guess I should say letter because I only read one before doing away with the entire box." She groaned.

"Were they that bad?"

"To describe it in a nutshell, I felt it was a vice or tool he was using to try to make up for lost time, maybe even to make up for what he did. I can't get past it, and I never will. There's not enough fame or money in the world that can come along and buy my love. It didn't work back then when he chose fame over family, and it certainly won't work for me now." She explained with strong conviction.

"I'm proud of you. I'm sure it wasn't easy arriving at that conclusion. The more I hear you talk about it, the more sorry I am for not just falling back and giving you the adequate space that you needed without all the added drama and pressure from a jealous boyfriend," he said, holding his head down.

Mackenzie slipped her hand over his. "There's nothing wrong with having a healthy amount of jealousy, you know. If I think about it, you had every right to question me. I should've come right out and told him to go fly a kite regarding any thoughts of us getting back together."

Brody chuckled.

"What's so funny?" she asked.

"Well, I have to give the guy a lot of credit. The nerve of him. He selfishly took off to fulfill his dreams, didn't show his face once while Stephanie was an itty bitty thing, and now he's back, just like that, buying a house on the Island and everything. If you ask me, I think he was banking on winning you over with his bank account. Either way, I'm glad you didn't fall for it. I think you'd do a lot better with a guy like me," he said, popping his collar and slicking his hair back.

Mackenzie's natural instincts caused her to give him a

playful shove, momentarily forgetting about his discomfort. "Ooh, I'm so sorry. Are you okay?"

"I'm fine. Note to self... never get too cocky or proud around Mackenzie Rowland. It may result in pain." They both laughed before settling down while gazing into each other's eyes.

"Do you think maybe you should get off your feet? We can go somewhere to talk further, you know," she said.

Brody looked in her eyes like a man would when he's longing to be with a woman. "I wish I could, but I don't trust myself to be alone with you tonight. You look beautiful in that dress, and I've missed you to the point where I find my mind wandering, thinking about things that only married folks should consider. So, I think it's best I call it a night while I'm ahead. My only goal is to do right by you."

The tingling sensation in her stomach was enough to make her feel weak in the knees.

"We may not be married yet, Brody, but that won't stop me from at least finishing the kiss we started earlier this evening."

Brody smiled. "I can agree to that. It was the sweetest kiss you'd ever given me. I didn't want it to end."

Mackenzie checked her watch as he pulled her closer, positioning her to lean on his body. "My watch tells me I have at least another hour to spare before I have to relieve the sitter. That's plenty of time to finish the kiss we started, wouldn't you say?"

Instead of answering, Brody engaged her fully in a half empty parking lot without a care in the world for who could see them.

CHAPTER 14

The following week Mae slid into a booth across from Meredith and Edith. They'd ordered her favorite apple pie while waiting for her arrival. To her surprise, girls' night was becoming a thing, and oddly enough, she found herself liking it.

"Ladies, don't look now. I think I found the perfect guy for Edith. I don't know why I didn't think of this before now," she said.

Edith slapped her hand down on the table, sending all kinds of warning signals to Mae. "Don't you dare. Just when I finally made up my mind that I'm fine without having a man in my life, now you want to introduce me. All men ever do is bring about heartache and pain. Besides, the new job at the boutique is keeping me busy. I don't have time."

Mae positioned herself against the comfortable, cushioned leather seats. "Baloney. This whole thing started because the two of you agreed you needed to get out of the house and meet people. My job was to be here for moral support and to introduce you. Now you don't want to meet anybody? Come on, Edith. What harm will it do?"

Meredith leaned in. "Tell me who he is. Is he sitting with the group over at four o'clock? Or is he sitting alone at the table located at six o'clock?" she whispered.

Edith relaxed the wrinkles in her forehead and stared at Meredith. "Four o'clock and six o'clock? Really, Meredith?"

"Yes, I heard the characters on my favorite daytime television show use the same lingo and I thought it was kind of cute. There's something about it that adds a little mystery to figuring out who it is." She smiled, sounding completely oblivious as to how silly it sounded.

"Ah ha. Well, do me a favor, let's change the subject all together. I'd much rather hear about how things are going with you and Theodore."

Mae held up her hand. "Not so fast. The evening is still young. There will be plenty of time to talk about Theodore in just a bit. However, I really think you need to step out of your own way. There's nothing wrong with at least saying hello."

"Edgar?" Meredith asked. "That's who you were referring to? Oh, Mae. You might want to find another guy. He has a history with women that's about a mile long and counting. Don't be fooled by the whole sweet grandpa appearance. He's way too friendly with all the women at our meetings. He's a hard pass in my opinion."

Mae hesitated, questioning Meredith at first, but then remembered she had a keen way of knowing everybody's business, particularly those among the HOA. "In that case, what about Fred Meyers, sitting at the counter, talking to Mackenzie? I'll bet he's a nice catch," she said, winking at Edith.

"Mae, thanks, but the answer is no. I'm sincere when I say that I don't need a man to make me happy. I'll admit, when I first moved here, I thought perhaps relocating would give me a fresh start and I'd be open to meeting someone. But, let the truth be told, I haven't healed from my first marriage. I don't know that I could ever go through something like that again. I wouldn't wish it on anybody."

Mae sighed. "Okay, up until now, I wasn't going to pry, but now I'm really curious to know. Outside of your typical infidelity after being married for several years, what really happened that has you so shut off to meeting someone new? And, by the way, I'm not making light of the fact that he cheated on you. But the way I see it, that's his loss, not yours."

"It sure is." Meredith chimed in.

Edith looked upward to the ceiling. "For heaven's sake. If only it were that easy. I find that every time I try to shove any attachment to my ex in the past, it always backfires on me. Take moving to Solomons for example. I briefly met a gentleman or two not long after I arrived, but I found myself just testing the waters to see if I still had it. I didn't really want anything other than a little attention. I'll bet anything that has everything to do with my abandonment issues."

Meredith placed her hand over Edith's. "Abandonment?" she asked.

Edith nodded. "Well, sure. When the man you've been married to for decades chooses every other woman but you… how should I feel?"

Mae interrupted. "That's terrible. You're beautiful, you're a wonderful homemaker, plus a kind friend. It's a shame you had to walk away feeling anything other than happy he's now out of your life."

"Yeah, well, unfortunately that's not how it works. When you find lipstick stains on your husband's collar after a long business trip, and smell the scent of another woman's perfume on his clothing, that's the moment reality sets in. After every unanswered call to his hotel room, and the concierge mistakenly admitting that he was out with Mrs. Meyer, even though I am Mrs. Meyer, so therefore he couldn't be out with me... after all of that for several years of marriage, the only thing that's left to feel is abandonment. I deserved better," she said.

Mae's heart sank, stealing her appetite to eat and desire to play matchmaker anymore.

"Gee, Edith. I'm sorry."

"There's no need to be sorry. It's just going to take time, that's all. One of the worst things I could ever do is jump into something else under the false pretense that I'm ready when I'm really not. The best thing I could ever do is stay true to my feelings, something I wasn't doing when I moved here or the evening when you introduced Meredith to Theodore. That part of Edith Meyers will have to change, starting now."

Meredith spoke in a low voice. "So, how did you find out all this was going on if he was away on business trips?"

"A woman has her ways. Especially nowadays since the invention of social media and all the other telltale warning signs I told you about. When I confronted him, I acted as if I'd already confirmed it was true. He tried to deny the allegations for a solid three hours, but as soon as I reminded him of how the cards were in my hands and how much alimony was at stake, he started crying like a big baby. Of course, by then, the damage had already been done." Edith explained.

Mae grunted out of pure disgust. It also made her think about whatever minor disagreements she'd recently had with Jonathan were peanuts in comparison. She'd rather do all that she could to create a happy life with Jonathan than go through anything like Edith had experienced.

"Man, oh man. Well, in that case, I don't blame you. Take as much time as you need. There's no rule about these things. I recently read in an article that people who find themselves single after once being a part of a happy marriage, let's say the spouse died, as was the case in my first marriage, then afterward it's a lot easier to meet somebody new. I don't know if that's entirely true because it took a long time for my heart to heal. But who knows. The article also said those coming out of a tumultuous relationship usually are hesitant to enter into a new one. I don't know if there's truth to any of it, but I do know this — if there was ever a time to take care of your emotional and mental well-being, then the time is now. No one deserves to go through what you experienced. Absolutely no one."

"Thank you, Mae. At times I consider going to see a therapist, but I haven't," Edith said.

Meredith looked shocked. "What are you waiting for? It would probably do you a lot of good, getting everything off your chest."

"Ha, I don't have a good reason. I assumed the feelings would dissipate over time, but surprisingly they haven't. However, that may change after tonight. Just sitting here talking to you ladies is already making a world of difference. I really am happy to have you as friends. It's the best gift Solomons Island has giving me thus far." Edith chuckled.

Mae nodded her head in agreement. "That makes two of us. I went around behaving like a grumpy old fart prior to starting this circle of friendship. What do you say we make a toast?" she asked.

Meredith picked up her glass of water. "A toast to what?"

"Oh, I know." Edith jumped in. "A toast to friendship and to Mae's five years until retirement... may it be the best five years ever... and finally a toast to new beginnings for you and Theodore."

"Wow, okay, that was a lot, but I'll toast to that," Mae said, joyfully tapping glasses, drawing in onlookers toward the center of the café.

CHAPTER 15

Mackenzie strolled down the concrete path of the annual art festival, walking with Stephanie, hand-in-hand. It was a neutral place for the two most important men in Stephanie's life to meet. However, that particular afternoon, Mack couldn't tell if she was sweating from the heat of the day or the mere idea that she was bringing Ben and Brody together. Either way, if she were going to properly tackle this next chapter in her life, she knew she'd have to start somewhere.

"Are you excited about Brody meeting your dad?" she asked.

"Yep, I'll bet dad could probably teach Brody how to play the guitar if he wanted to learn."

Mackenzie smiled, adoring her sweet daughter's innocence and willingness to love. "I'm not sure, baby. I think we'll have to give them time to figure out their relationship. Sometimes grown-ups take a little longer to make friends, and since your dad and Brody don't really know each other, you may need to give them a little time."

"Time to decide if they can be friends? That's the silliest thing I've ever heard," Stephanie said.

"Hmm, it may sound silly, but I'm sure you can recall times when you weren't sure if you would hit it off with a new friend. Maybe you were feeling afraid or nervous that you might not have anything in common or get along."

She watched as Stephanie wrinkled her eyebrows, contemplating what she was saying.

Stephanie broke her silence. "Yep, that happened to me before. But I know it won't be that way with Dad and with Brody. They're both really nice, and they already have something in common."

"What's that, love?"

"They both care about you and me. Duh, Mommy, everybody knows that." She giggled.

"Stephanie Rowland, you are well beyond your years, young lady. How about we stop by Aunt Agnes' food truck to say hello before we meet the guys?"

"Okay."

After passing several tables of abstract and vintage art, Mackenzie turned a corner, bumping right into Clara. "Mack, I didn't expect to see you and Stephanie here. What a pleasant surprise," she said.

Mack shifted her attention toward Stephanie. "Trust me, this was definitely a last-minute plan, wasn't it, Steph?"

"Yeah, Dad only has a couple of days in town before he has to get back on the road again."

Clara seemed slightly surprised but played along. "Oh, I see. Spending more time with your dad these days? That sounds like loads of fun."

Mackenzie winked at Clara. "Actually, today is a really big day because Brody will join us as well. He'll get to meet Steph's dad for the first time. Isn't that right, love?"

"Yep," Steph said, looking up at her mom.

Clara chuckled. "A first time meeting at the art festival, in broad daylight, where everyone can see you. Ha, that's actually a smart idea." She winked.

"Now, now, Clara. Behave yourself. I'm sure their first-time gathering will be just fine. We were actually going to look for Agnes' bbq truck so we could stop by and say hello. Is she here today?" Mackenzie asked.

Clara pointed, giving them directions to the truck. Without saying much, Mackenzie could read her body language, knowing she was beyond curious about how the day's events would unfold. "Perfect. We're going to head down now, and then perhaps circle back when the guys arrive. Will you be here for a little while?"

"I'll return toward the end of the festival to help Agnes clean up. For now, I need to head back to the office and help Mike with a huge project. If we don't see each other later this afternoon, call me later. I'm dying to hear how everything turns out." Again, she winked, and gave Mack and Steph a quick hug.

At the food truck Agnes was a natural, serving ribs with her sidekick Grant. An unexpected sight to see, but one that was welcomed.

"Agnes and Grant, well, well. Don't you two look cute operating the food truck together." Mack teased.

"Thank you, but my help called out sick today. I'm sure Grant would much rather be eating my food than serving, isn't that right?" She glanced lovingly at Grant who agreed.

"She's right, but I have a few hours to spare before my meeting this afternoon, so I figured why not come out and help. It's the least I can do since Agnes is always cooking for me and trying to fatten me up." He laughed.

Mack observed the way he snuck in quick kisses in between

their banter, giving her the warm fuzzies that they were so happy and in love.

"Well, Steph and I just wanted to stop by and say hello. We ran into Clara and told her that later on maybe we'd stop by with her dad and Brody to pick something up for dinner. That's, of course, if you don't run out of food by then. Word has spread pretty quickly about how popular your food truck is."

"Aww, thanks, Mack. You guys are welcome to come by anytime. And don't worry. Whatever you want to order, we can whip it up on the grill in no time. Stephanie, I'll even save one of our most popular desserts just for you." Agnes promised.

"Yay, thank you."

∽

By the time Brody texted from the parking lot confirming his arrival, Ben was already walking toward her with a bouquet of red roses in hand. *Please tell me the flowers are for Stephanie.*

But, instead, he offered the roses to her with his hand outstretched and then revealed a yellow bouquet to Stephanie from behind his back.

Oh, good Lord. Mackenzie continued with an awkward smile. She didn't want to take away from her daughter's joy, but what was he thinking? Wasn't the yellow bouquet for Steph more than enough?

"Well, aren't you two looking lovely today?" Ben said.

Mack nudged Stephanie. "What do you say for the flowers?"

"Thanks, Dad. The flowers are beautiful," she said, beaming from ear to ear.

"Pretty flowers for the pretty ladies, of course. I wouldn't have it any other way."

Before Mack could say thanks, Brody showed up, standing beside him. "You must be Ben Rowland," he said, extending his hand.

Ben returned the handshake. "Hey, buddy, how did you guess?"

Brody glanced over at the red flowers in Mack's hand, then sized Ben up. "Some things are just easy to figure out."

Amid a humid afternoon with enough steam in the air to make it difficult to breathe, Mackenzie found herself holding in her breath, hoping Brody would be the bigger man, choosing to ignore the gesture from Ben.

"Hey there, sweet girl. It's been a while. How are you?" Brody asked, gently bending to give Stephanie a hug.

"I'm fine. I missed you, Brody. Is your back feeling better?" she asked.

"It's going to be a while before I feel one hundred percent, but I have a really good doctor who's working on me. Guess what?"

Stephanie bounced to her tippy toes and back down in anticipation of what he would say. "What?"

He spoke in a low voice. "I also brought a special surprise for you. I have it in the car. Remind me to give it to you before we leave."

"Okay," she whispered back.

Mackenzie cleared her throat. "Gentlemen, I believe a proper introduction is in order. You're both here because you mean a lot to Stephanie and me," she said, mostly looking toward Brody at the end.

"Over the last month or so she has repeatedly asked me when would Brody meet her dad. So, I'd like Stephanie to have the honor of introducing you." Then she paused. "Go ahead, baby."

"Dad, this is Brody, and Brody this is Dad," she said, followed by an impromptu curtsey to which both men smiled.

"Great. Now that we have that behind us, why don't we check out the kids' art section? Maybe while we're walking there, you can tell Brody and Dad about our visit to the cliffs."

While the four of them strolled, Mack glanced at Brody as he attentively listened. She found herself wanting to be either at home, or on this excursion alone, without Ben, but she at least appreciated how Brody was getting along. One of the many reasons she loved him so much.

"Hey, baby, there's a beautiful painting of your favorite sea turtles. Why don't you go over and take a look? Maybe you can find a painting just right for your room."

"Okay." She placed the bouquet in her dad's hands and ran off to check out the art.

Mack's shoulders shifted as she faced both men head on. "Okay, before Stephanie comes back, there's something that's eating me up inside and needs to be addressed."

"I'm listening," Ben said.

"We're here because it's important, not only to Stephanie that you meet Brody because she loves him so much, but to me as well, because this man is going to be my future husband."

Ben reared his head back. "I guess congratulations are in order. I didn't realize you two were that serious."

Mack held her finger up. "Don't do that, Ben. What we had was many moons ago, and even then, you fell very short. I already expressed to you how much Brody means to me. Therefore, showing up with red roses was a bit inappropriate, and maybe even somewhat deliberate, but either way, very unnecessary."

"Okay," he said.

"Now, for Stephanie's sake, I want us to all get along,

harmoniously, which shouldn't be too difficult to do since we all have one common goal, which is —"

Ben threw his hands up. "Stephanie, I get it. Don't worry. I don't plan on being a thorn in your side or putting a damper in your plans with lover boy over here."

"Ben!" she said, noticing Brody roll his eyes.

"Sorry, I'll admit I returned here with high hopes for something more. But it's clear you two have something that's already been established, so you don't have to worry about me getting in the way. All I want is what's best for Steph, and for me that's living close by so I can spend time with her when I'm not on the road, and well —"

Ben gave Brody the once over. "If you're as good as Mack says you are, which you must be because Mack has very good judgement, then I want you to be in Stephanie's life as well."

Interesting. Mack thought. After all, Ben went from being a deadbeat dad to feeling comfortable enough to suggest who should be a part of Stephanie's life.

What did I ever see in this guy again? She thought to herself.

Brody piped up. "Look, man, I don't want anything but good for your daughter and for Mackenzie for that matter. That's all I've ever been about from day one. I can't say that I was thrilled to learn about you pursuing Mack, but she's a gem, so I completely understand the temptation. Let's just be clear, now that we've had this little talk. I'm assuming you'll respect our relationship boundaries, and that we'll keep our personal interaction respectful at all times, especially for Stephanie's sake," he said, then extended his hand for Ben's acceptance.

Mackenzie counted to ten, holding her breath for what felt like longer than she should've. But, as she watched, Ben finally placed his hand in Brody's, giving him a hearty handshake just in time for Stephanie's return.

Mackenzie relaxed as she watched the guys escort Stephanie to Agnes' food truck. Following closely behind, she wanted to pinch herself, having a hard time imagining a day like this could ever exist.

It was clear her initial wavering over Ben was nothing more than her old self crying out for closure. But nothing and no one could ever replace the love she had for Brody. Not now, not ever.

Agnes leaned out of the window. "There you are, Stephanie. I was starting to wonder if you and mom would ever return." She smiled. This time, instead of Grant being behind the counter, Clara was by her side, looking ever so curious to check out Ben.

"I told you I would be back. We're so hungry we could order the whole menu, right Mom?" Stephanie asked.

"Uh, I'm not sure about the whole menu, love. How about we start with some barbecue chicken? And, before we do that, how about you politely go around back and give your Aunt Clara and your Aunt Agnes a hug." Mack instructed.

"Okay."

Mack watched as Clara acknowledged Brody. She then slid by Brody's side and held her hand toward Ben. "Ladies, this is Ben, Stephanie's dad."

Agnes waved. "Hi, Stephanie's dad. Word around town is you're a talented rockstar. I'll confess I've never heard your music, but if you're good enough to play at National Harbor, then I think you ought to set up something for the residents of Solomons Island to enjoy." She giggled, then bent down out of sight, presumably giving Stephanie a hug.

Ben blushed at the attention. "I'm not sure about the rockstar part. I'm just a guy who knows his way around a guitar and is able to hold a note or two. No big deal."

Clara on the other hand just watched him, more like a parent who was uncertain of the new guy's motives. "Brody, how's that back of yours coming along? I can imagine being on your feet for a long time has to be taking its toll," she said.

"Oh, it's likely that I'll need to soak in a hot tub of water tonight, but to see this little girl happy was well worth it," he replied, smiling at Stephanie who'd returned.

"Mmm, that sounds like something you would do." Then she shifted her attention toward Ben. "The one thing you can always count on, when you're busy traveling on your tours, is that Brody will always be here. He's been a constant staple in Steph's life. In all our lives for that matter."

Mack held her head down. *Oh, dear.* She thought to herself, then redirected the conversation. "So, ladies, how about that barbecue chicken platter? I'll take two, one for me and Steph to go. Gentlemen, would you like to go ahead and place your orders?"

Brody stepped forward. "I'll have the rack of ribs and potato salad on the side. Once Ben is done placing his order, put everything on one tab," he said, passing his card through the window.

Mack shook her head, doing everything not to laugh at Clara's overprotective gesture.

~

That evening Mackenzie hummed to herself as she closed the door to Stephanie's room. It was a sweet sound that Brody missed and longed to hear again. He glanced at her curvature and long dangling locks as she approached him with a smile, then patted his lap.

"Do you think that's such a smart idea? I don't want to cause any additional aches and pains."

He laughed. "My lap works just fine, but my heart will be broken if you don't come on over here and sit with me."

"Well, I certainly have no intentions of being a heartbreaker," she said, making herself comfortable.

His blue eyes met hers.

"Thank you for what you did earlier today, going above and beyond to make your feelings for me known to Ben. It meant a lot."

Mack cupped her hands gently around his cheeks. "Brody, you deserve so much more than a declaration of my love at an art festival. I should've been that intentional right from the start."

"Shh." He placed his finger over her lips. "You don't have to speak another word of apology, Mackenzie. After having time to think through everything, I was the one being selfish. What was I to expect when a man you'd committed your life to and had a child with returned making a case for getting back together? I bet you had so many unanswered questions... so many emotions you were fighting, probably partially wanting to wring his neck, while also wanting an explanation all at the same time. I was jealous and foolish. I promise that will never happen again."

Mack playfully kissed the finger he used to shush her with. "We could go back and forth all evening about how we could've done a better job at handling ourselves, but how about we press forward with something way more important."

"What's that?"

"Remember our conversation about planning for the future?"

Brody's mustache curled upward as he smiled really big.

"How could I forget?" He swept his hand around her waist, pulling her closer in.

"I was hoping you'd be open to the idea of having a sit down with Stephanie. After observing the way she's been handling herself over these last few weeks, I honestly think she's ready. It almost amazes me that she hasn't shown one ounce of anger or bitterness toward Ben, and that she still had such an open heart toward you, and us collectively as a couple. It's like all she sees is love. That's it. No level of bitterness or uncertainty, no expectations for Ben and me to get back together... just love. It's to the point where I was still considering having the kid checked out by a shrink, just to make sure she's okay."

Brody rested his head back, chuckling in pure amusement. "Ha, why does there have to be something wrong with her? I think we as adults take for granted just how much they understand it. She may never be able to express her feelings the way we can, but I'll bet she's even more discerning than we are. Plus, if you're that concerned about what's going on in that pretty little mind of hers, why don't you just ask her?"

She hadn't considered it before now, but Mackenzie had been very delicate and cautious with Stephanie. Maybe it was time she came right out and bluntly asked her thoughts.

"That's part of what I wanted to discuss with you. I was thinking we both could have a sit down with her, letting her know that we're planning —"

Brody lifted his head. "Planning to get engaged soon?"

Hearing the words set the rhythm of her heartbeat out of sync. Her eyes wandered from his eyes down to his chest and back. "Yes," she said in a soft voice.

Feeling the palm of his hand rise up the center of her back, pulling her gently to lie on his chest gave her goosebumps, sending chills up her spine.

Brody spoke while stroking her hair in place. "Let's set an agreed upon day this week. Maybe fix a nice family meal, her favorite desert, and then talk with her and see how she feels about it. How does that sound?"

Mack let out a sigh of relief. "It sounds perfect."

CHAPTER 16

Mackenzie, Clara, and Agnes sat in a row with their feet stretched out, talking as they received foot massages and pedicures. Around mid-week, Solomons Beauty Salon was a quiet place the ladies could talk, or rather, question Mackenzie about every little detail of her love life.

"Okay, where do I begin?" Mack explained.

Clara raised her hand. "How about we rewind this baby all the way back to, I don't know, the moment when Ben showed up and totally rocked your world! Ever since he showed up on Solomons Island it's been nothing but one big tumultuous ride, if you ask me. The only thing good that's come from all this is finally seeing you and Brody back on track." She fussed.

Agnes waved. "Amen and hallelujah to that. Besides, the rockstar has absolutely nothing on Brody. I'd take humble and sexy all day, every day. There's nothing like having a man who can be satisfied living a peaceful life on the Island rather than one who's used to having groupies chasing after him all the time."

Mackenzie laughed uncontrollably. "You two are so bad. I

never got the impression that Ben is caught up in living the life of a celebrity with groupies following him everywhere he goes. Instead, I picked up on quite the opposite. He seems to have a lot of regrets for walking away on what we once had. He even made an effort to get us back, but, of course, that ship has long sailed for me." She explained.

"The nerve. I'm sorry, but I didn't like him from the start. Any man that walks away from a good woman like you isn't worth a hill of beans in my opinion." Clara expressed.

Agnes chuckled. "Beans, Clara? Really?"

Clara sat upright. "You get my point."

Mackenzie made every effort to settle the uproar, feeling thankful it was just them in the salon. "Look, ladies, you might as well get used to the idea of Ben being somewhat of a regular on the Island. He's settled in his new home and plans on spending time with Stephanie whenever he can."

Clara continued fussing. "See, even that bothers me. When he can? When he can? It's amazing how he gets the option of being a part-time dad when you have been a full-time mother for all these years. You don't get time off from being a parent. If you ask me, he's still putting his career first, don't you think?"

Mackenzie sighed, not really able to get a word in edgewise.

Clara continued. "This is the last thing I'll say. I'm so grateful you have Brody in your life. He's a real man, demonstrating nothing but genuine love for the both of you, full-time, right from the start. If you would've mentioned a word about going back to Ben, I would've been prepared to let you have it." She huffed, leaning back in her chair.

Mack closed her eyes as the technician covered her legs with a hot towel rub. "I couldn't agree with you more. I always knew I loved Brody, but this whole ordeal sent me into a tailspin for a while. Thankfully, I have mental clarity and I'm ready to move forward."

She kept her eyes closed, drifting to thoughts of last night envisioning Brody as he held her close to his chest, making her feel secure in their relationship.

"Wait, move forward as in —?" Agnes asked.

Mack smiled. "As in talking with Stephanie about taking the next step. I'm already nervous about it, so let's talk about something else, and I'll update you after we have the talk. What about you? How's things going with Grant? You two look so natural together. I wouldn't be surprised if you're not walking down the aisle soon."

Mackenzie felt a tap on her arm from Agnes, who sat in the middle. "For the record, you have nothing to be nervous about. From what I can tell, it's obvious Stephanie adores Brody," she said.

Clara chimed in. "I second the motion. He's the perfect fit and she'll be over the moon at the idea of the two of you getting married. And, before Ag tells you about Grant, I just want you to know that any frustration you may have heard out of me yesterday was only because I love you and would do anything to protect you, Mack. I hope you know that."

Mack raised up, looking at Clara. "You know I feel the same way, friend."

The two had been there for each other from the moment Clara arrived on the Island, seeking a fresh start. She knew the sisterly love ran deep and didn't mind that Clara had her back.

"Okay, Agnes. What's going on with you and the writer? You two do a lot of kissing, but you never tell. Spill the beans, already." Mack teased.

Agnes smiled. "A lady never kisses and tells, but I can say that we're writing our own little love story and so far, the plot continues to thicken."

Mackenzie didn't know whether to laugh or playfully bop her over the head with a magazine. "I want details. What's he like? Is he romantic? Or does he save all the romance for his novels? Do you love him? Does he love you? Come on, spill it."

Agnes appeared to be getting a kick out of the high level of interest. "Wow, okay, hold on a minute. One question at a time. Starting with the first, he's brilliant. He captivates my mind with intriguing ideas and theories on life that I've never heard of before. This is the first time I've ever been with somebody who challenges me intellectually and I think it's very —"

"Sexy?" Clara asked.

"Yes, that's the perfect way to describe it."

Mackenzie poked fun. "Oh, yeah, she's hooked."

"Hey, you asked, so I'm telling you. Let's see, is he romantic? I'd say romance is his primary love language if there is such a thing. That, and of course, physical touch."

"Whoaaa." The ladies sang in unison.

"No, no, no. Not like that. Trust me when I tell you, we're behaving ourselves. But he's affectionate, spontaneous, and extremely thoughtful, which of course for me, is a very good recipe for romance."

"I'm happy for you, Ag. To think you almost missed out on all of this because of your ridiculous sabbatical." Clara teased.

"Hey, I had good intentions at the time. It just so happens that things didn't go according to plan."

Mack laughed. "Mmm hmm, well, I too am happy for you just like Clara. Now, we better hurry up and get these nails polished if I plan on making it back to the café on time. If I show up one minute beyond the time I promised Joshua, I'll never hear the end of it."

CHAPTER 17

Mae dragged what appeared to be a large picture frame draped in a sheet across the living room floor. She hoped not to disturb Jonathan, but instead surprise him when he joined her downstairs for dinner.

"Looks like somebody purchased the largest painting they had for sale," he said, nearly scaring the daylights out of her.

"Jonathan! You could at least warn me for goodness' sake."

The smirk on his face revealed suspicion as he stood on the bottom of the stairwell in his robe.

"Warn you about what? I live here and since you're the one coming in from the art festival, I doubt you needed much warning that I'd be home," he said, pointing toward the draped frame. "What do you have there?"

Mae smiled and looked down at the sheet as if she was proud of what was underneath. "It's a gift for you. I picked up something that I thought would speak to your heart in a really big way. As I was passing by, this painting reminded me of you, and I just couldn't leave it behind. Would you like to see it?"

"Would I? I don't think I've ever owned a work of art

before. I always relied on decorations from the local home store. Wait," he said, stopping in his tracks. "How much did this set us back? From what I hear, artwork can be rather expensive."

She held her stomach, laughing hard enough for her belly to jiggle. "Oh, Jonathan, how tacky. You're not supposed to ask how much your gift costs. Trust me when I tell you that I didn't break the bank. Now, come on over here and open up your gift. I'm dying to know what you think."

Jonathan watched as Mae removed the ivory sheet, revealing a picture of a home with a Floridian landscape, a white picket fence, and palm trees. "What's this?" he asked with his eyes lit up like a child in an amusement park.

"It's a rendition of our retirement home. The one we'll have built when we move to Florida in five years."

She watched as Jonathan stood back taking it all in, pointing to the palm trees and admiring its beauty. He looked at her and chuckled. "Are you serious, Mae?"

"Very serious. I've been thinking about it more and more each day. Then, this afternoon as I was strolling through the fair, this painting jumped out at me like a sign from above. The truth is, I can be happy just about anywhere, as long as I'm with you, Jonathan. If Florida is where you want to be, then that's where I want to be as well."

He stood back with slightly teary eyes as if he were in total disbelief. "I don't even know where to begin, Mae. You never cease to amaze me."

"How about you begin by deciding where you'd like to hang the painting? We may not live in this exact house, but I figured until moving day comes, we can hang it somewhere, giving ourselves something exciting to look forward to. What do you say?"

Jonathan picked up the painting, holding it up to one of the walls in the living room. "Did you have a specific place in mind?"

"It could go above the couch if you'd like," she replied.

He leaned the frame against the wall, inviting her to come closer with open arms. "How did I get to be this lucky? The sacrifices you've made for the sake of our marriage —"

Mae interrupted. "You mean the sacrifices we've made for each other. That's what love is supposed to be. Not one man or woman for himself or herself. But both husband and wife looking out for the other, no?"

He smiled. "I've been thinking about this whole thing just as much as you. Last year I was bent on having my way with purchasing the boat so we could travel. Perhaps this year I should be bent on figuring out our finances so that within the next five years we can just make sure this place is paid off so we can stay. I haven't said it out loud, but I've been pondering the idea when I lie in bed at night."

"Now, hold on. The only thing you're supposed to be pondering when you lie in bed at night is having a romantic evening with me. That explains why you've been so deep in thought. I was starting to think you weren't interested in me anymore." She teased.

"Woman, you ought to know me better than that."

Still smiling, Mae released her arms from around his waist and walked over to the painting, grazing her fingers across the dried paint strokes. "It sounds like the two of us are going out of our way to ensure the other is happy, but at some point, a decision will have to be made. I say we hang the painting up and let it be inspiration for the life we look forward to building together in retirement. Just know that I'm sincere, Jonathan. As long as I'm with you, I'll be happy. Every time you look at this painting, I want you to remember that, okay?"

Jonathan drew close behind and eased his hands around

her waistline. He softly kissed her, giving her a chill along her neckline. "How about tonight we table the discussion? Instead, I'd like to show you just how much I'm still interested in you, Mae Middleton. The painting will be here when we rise in the morning."

Mae tilted her head back, letting out joyful laughter. "You are terrible, Jonathan. Absolutely terrible."

"And you like every single bit of it." He teased.

~

"How do you like Brody's idea for Beach Saturdays during the month of August, Steph?" Mackenzie asked as she and Brody set up their beach chairs and large umbrella.

"I love it! From now on, every single Saturday in August is Beach Saturday, all the way until school re-opens. It's a genius idea!" She smiled.

Brody pitched the umbrella in the sand and stood back, looking proud of his work. "You know what, Steph, we need somebody to be in charge of meal planning for Beach Saturdays. Do you think that can be a task that I hand over to you?"

"Sure. Mom likes turkey sandwiches, I like chicken cutlets, and Brody, yours is easy. You'll eat anything. At least that's what Mom says." She laughed.

Mackenzie shook her head and raised her hand to her side. "Gee, thanks, kiddo. That was supposed to be a little joke between the two of us."

"Oops," Steph replied.

Brody spread their beach towels close to their chairs. "Well, it's not like mom wasn't telling the truth. I'm pretty easy-going. Another idea I had is perhaps you'd like to invite a friend for next week. You know, someone who likes to build sandcastles and design cool things in the sand just as much as you do."

"Okay, don't worry. I have plenty of friends I can invite." Mackenzie thrusted a beach ball in the air toward Stephanie, finding much amusement at watching her go after it. Her little girl was not so little anymore as she prepared to enter the third grade, was old enough to pick out her own outfits for the day, and was fast at retrieving their beach balls in the sand.

"So, love. Out of all the activities you've done this summer, which one has been your favorite?" Mack asked.

Steph thought about it for a moment before pitching the ball back. "Umm, it would have to be going to day camp, and going to the art festival with you, Brody, and Dad. But if I could only pick one, the art festival would be my favorite."

Mackenzie caught the beach ball, then paused. "Really? You'd choose the art festival over going to camp? Why is that, love?"

"It's easy. The art festival was the first time I had my whole family together in one place. It made me feel really special."

Mackenzie glanced over at Brody, who was already sitting on a lounge chair, while digging in the cooler for something to drink. "Did you hear that, Brody? If that wasn't a perfect lead in, then I don't know what is."

Brody chuckled. "I'd have to agree. Why don't the two of you come join me under the umbrella so we can settle in and eat."

Mack and Stephanie walked over and ducked under the umbrella. "What's a lead in?" Steph asked.

Brody winked at Mack, signaling that he'd take the first question. "Well, I think what your mother is trying to say is we're glad you had such a good time with your family at the festival. More importantly, I'm glad that you consider me as someone who is a part of your family."

"Oh," Steph replied, digging feverishly with her shovel to cover her feet with sand.

Mackenzie took a turn. "Stephanie, there's more, love. We were going to wait until after we ate, but since you brought up the topic of being a family, we'd like to talk to you about the three of us being a family. We know your dad is back in our lives now, and hopefully that will never change. But, how do you feel about Brody and I —" She paused, smiling toward Brody.

Stephanie, being the intuitive young lady that she was, completed Mackenzie's sentence, "Getting married? If you and Brody get married, does this mean I would officially have two dads?"

"Yes, that's exactly what it would mean. Of course, Brody would technically be your stepdad, but —" Mackenzie paused, temporarily at a loss for words.

Brody covered Mackenzie's hand with his own, gently filling in wherever she couldn't, working harmoniously together like a symphony. "I would be your stepdad, which means that I'd still offer you all the love in the world as if you were my very own. I'd never try to take the place of your real father, but I'd promise to be there for you, and your mother, supporting you both in every way that I know how."

Mack signaled Brody with a smile and waited for Steph to process everything they were saying. This was a big moment for them collectively. The last time Mack had to make such a big decision was the day she packed up their belongings and moved to Solomons Island, and of course, the day she accepted Ben back into their lives, which wasn't that long ago.

"I'm happy that you're marrying my mom, Brody." She looked up and smiled.

Brody let out a hearty laugh, more like his version of releasing nervous energy. Mack, on the other hand, could still see an air of concern in her baby's eyes.

"What's on your mind, Steph?"

"I wonder who Dad will get to marry someday. If you and Brody get married, then who's going to marry Dad and become my stepmom? And would she try to take me away to live with her and Dad?" Steph pondered.

Mackenzie's heart sank. "No, baby. No one is going to try and take you away. I know that our family is changing from what we've always known, but you aren't going anywhere. And if the day comes when your father meets someone and decides to marry her, that doesn't change what we have right now. Do you hear me?"

"Mmm hmm."

Mack bent down and held her by the shoulders. "It's very important to Brody and me that we discuss this with you first. How you feel means everything to us, love. The only thing that will change is, after the wedding we'll all live together. Everything else will remain the same."

Brody joined them in the sand. "I was kind of hoping you'd help me with a very important job."

"What is it?" she asked.

"Picking out a ring for your mother. Do you think you could help me? It's a pretty big responsibility."

A huge smiled was smeared across Stephanie's face. "Sure! I'm really good at picking out jewelry. Mom says I always pick out the most expensive pieces." Steph giggled.

Brody's eyes met Mackenzie's. "Oh, boy. We might have to give her another task." He teased.

"Say there, Stephanie... how much do you know about planning a proposal?"

The three joked around and made history as they celebrated their first Beach Saturday in August. Hopefully, next year this time, they'd celebrate their new tradition as a family of three, or maybe even more, should Mack and Brody ever decide to grow their family.

CHAPTER 18

Mackenzie wiped down the counter at the café, clearing the way for her next customer as Clara, Agnes, and Mae joined her for lunch.

"Ladies, you should've been there. Brody and I had the sweetest conversation with Steph this weekend about us getting married. I was so proud of the way he handled himself with her. That man has truly been nothing short of a blessing in my life."

Clara dabbed her eyes with a napkin. "Your love story is so sweet. I wish you two nothing but many years of happiness."

Mack snickered to herself. "Thank you, love. Feeling a little emotional, are we? Why the sudden tears?"

"Oh, everything is fine. I'm just a sucker for a good love story, that's all," Clara said.

Mae nodded in agreement. "I'm starting to think there's something about the Island that brings people together. Think about it. Jonathan and I came here as friends but became husband and wife. Clara, you met Mike at Lighthouse Tours. Agnes fell in love with an author who wasn't even from here.

And now there's Mackenzie and Brody. At this point I'm convinced there has to be something in the water on Solomons Island for sure."

Mack chuckled. "Yeah, it's called good seafood. That's what we're known for. Good seafood and good men."

Mackenzie thrived when she was among friends and loved ones at the café. Today, in particular, the place was packed with familiar faces gathered in every corner, dining and laughing together. The sound was like music to her ears. "Ladies, speaking of good men, looks like we talked him up. There's Brody coming in now with Mike. Gee, we don't normally all gather here at the same time like this. Not unless there's a special occasion. I better go tell Chef Harold to keep the specials coming. He's really starting to draw a big crowd."

She noticed Clara and Agnes exchanging looks but didn't pay it much mind as Brody entered the front door. "Mack, I think you better stay here for a moment. You probably don't want to miss this." She winked.

"Hey, everybody!" Brody announced.

Mackenzie was startled by a subtle tap on the back of her arm.

"Stephanie? How did you get here? You're supposed to be at home with the sitter."

"Chef Harold let me in through the back door. He called home and said it was time to come for the special surprise."

It hit Mackenzie as clear as day that everyone was up to something. It actually made more sense with practically all of Lighthouse Tours there, in addition to their friends from the neighborhood.

Brody took Mack by the hand and led her from behind the counter. "Come with me."

She followed, glancing over at her friends, who were anxiously holding their hands up to their mouths. In that moment, Mack knew what was about to happen. She suspected her old-fashioned man had gathered everyone so he could propose. Brody liked to do things in a humble way, and so did she, therefore a proposal with those they loved made the most sense.

He stopped in the center of the café. "Now, Mack, before you say anything. I realize there were a million ways that I could've gone about this. On Monday, Steph's sitter was kind enough to bring her to the jewelry store to meet me before going to the park. I needed my sidekick to help me pick out something really special for you."

By now, the crowd was silent. You couldn't hear a thing, not even the sound of one fork scraping across a plate.

Brody continued. "Please don't be mad at the babysitter. It was important to me that Steph be a part of this occasion, just like it was important for me to do this today before our friends here as our witnesses. I chose the café because this place means so much to you... to us. It's not only where we first met, but the place where I asked you out on our first date, and you said yes."

Brody bent down on one knee and pulled a box from his back pocket. "Having you and Stephanie in my life has brought me nothing short of pure, unspeakable joy. The kind of joy I'd like to experience for the rest of my life, if you would allow me the honor."

He opened the box, exposing a shiny round diamond with a halo of smaller diamonds all around it.

"I knew you were the one the moment you risked everything and jumped in the Patuxent River with me." He smiled.

In the background, she could hear Stephanie whispering, "Mommy jumped in the river?" To which the crowd laughed.

Brody removed the ring and held it before her. "Mackenzie Rowland, will you marry me?"

"Yes! Yes, yes, yes," she said, holding out her hand as he slid the diamond on her ring finger. "Oh my goodness, I can't believe this! You got me so good." She laughed.

Brody stood and hugged her tightly and lifted her off the ground. "I guess this means we're officially engaged."

As they kissed, Clara nestled next to Mike. Jonathan, who'd quietly slipped in, gathered next to Mae, and Joshua, her employee, slipped a coin in the jutebox, selecting a song, inviting all the patrons to celebrate with the happy couple.

A new Solomons book will be available in the near future. In the meantime, are you ready to try a new beach series? CLICK here or turn the page to learn more about Tropical Encounter. A new Tropical Breeze series!

ALSO BY MICHELE GILCREST

When Meg Carter advances a year's worth of rent on a new Bohemian beach house, she's shocked to land and discover the place has been sold at an auction.

The new owner, Parker Wilson, is forty, a real estate investor, and ready to get the property flip underway. When Meg digs her heels in and refuses to leave, will this drive them to become enemies? Or will they find common ground and potentially become lovers?

After an end to a long engagement, all Meg wants out of life is a fresh start. She can't think of a better way to begin than by advancing her career in the hotel industry. When an opportunity comes along to accept a position at a five-star resort, she secures a beach rental, packs her bags, and heads to the Bahamas.

Meg's faith leads her to believe there's hope for the future after her fiancée of three years kicks her to the curb. But, will she face more heartache and disappointment when she discovers she has nowhere to live?

Tropical Encounter is a clean beach read with a touch of inspiration that's sure to give you all the feels.

Pull up your favorite beach chair and watch as Meg and Parker's story unfold!

Click here to order today!

Printed in Great Britain
by Amazon